PETER PAN

or

The Boy Who Would Not Grow Up

A Fantasy in Five Acts

BY J.M. BARRIE

IN A NEW VERSION BY
JOHN CAIRD & TREVOR NUNN

★

★

DRAMATISTS
PLAY SERVICE
INC.

CUL262

PETER PAN or The Boy Who Would Not Grow Up
Copyright © 1993, John Caird and Trevor Nunn
Copyright © 1985, John Caird and Trevor Nunn
as an unpublished dramatic composition

All Rights Reserved

SPECIAL NOTE

NOTE ON ORIGINAL MUSIC

For information and availability concerning the original music written by Stephen Oliver which was used in the London production, please contact G. Schirmer, Inc., Business Rental and Performance Department, P.O. Box 572, 445 Bellvale Road, Chester, New York 10918. Attn: Ella Windfield. Telephone: 845-469-2271. Facsimile: 845-469-7544.

for Stephen

... the utterly exhilarating new production by John Caird and Trevor Nunn at the Barbican. Gone is that simplified and often tacky Peter Pantomime we have endured in recent years past. Instead we have a resonant and beguiling fantasy that boasts as much spectacle as any child could wish; and that, at the same time, touches on the double Barriesque tragedy of growing up into conformity or being marooned indefinitely in the Never Land.

THE GUARDIAN

The first thing to be said about this irresistible production for the RSC by John Caird and Trevor Nunn is that I am amazed that the travesty tradition in the central role ... has survived so long ...

THE FINANCIAL TIMES

... The RSC has taken the work out of mothballs and elevated it from the ghetto of children's theatre into a national masterpiece.

THE TIMES

PETER PAN was first produced at the Barbican Theatre, the Royal Shakespeare Company's London, England, home, in London, England, on December 10, 1982. It was directed by John Caird and Trevor Nunn; the set design was by John Napier; the costume design was by Andreane Neofitou; the lighting design was by David Hersey and the music was by Stephen Oliver. The cast was as follows:

THE STORYTELLER	Stephen Moore
MR. DARLING	Joss Ackland
MRS. DARLING	Sheila Hancock
WENDY, AGE 12	Jane Carr
JOHN, AGE 10	Philip Franks
MICHAEL, AGE 6	Andrew Thomas James
NANA	Christopher Hurst
LIZA	Clare Travers-Deacon
PETER PAN	Miles Anderson
TINKER BELL	Jan Revere
THE OSTRICH	Susan Jane Tanner & Antony Simons
SLIGHTLY	James Fleet
TOOTLES	Anthony O'Donnell
NIBS	Joseph Marcell
CURLY	Dexter Fletcher
FIRST TWIN	Phillip Walsh
SECOND TWIN	Ken Robertson
CECCO	Steve Simmonds
BILL JUKES	Andrew Jarvis
COOKSON	Brian Poyser
GENTLEMAN STARKEY	Colin Tarrant
SKYLIGHTS	Stewart Mackintosh
SMEE	George Raistrick
NOODLER	Gary Sharkey
ROBERT MULLINS	Peter Ellis
CAPT. JAMES HOOK	Joss Ackland
THE CROCODILE	Andrew Jarvis & Steve Simmonds

GREAT BIG LITTLE PANTHER .... Mike Murray
TIGER LILY... Seeta Indrani
THE PICCANINNY TRIBE .... Sarah Finch, Noelyn George,
        Michael Gyngell, Tom Hunsinger, Christopher Hurst,
        Susan Leong, Antony Simons, Jan Revere, Susan Jane
                        Tanner, Clare Travers-Deacon
THE MERMAIDS .... Sarah Finch, Noelyn George,
           Susan Leong, Jan Revere, Susan Jane Tanner
THE NEVER BIRD .... Noelyn George
CHAY TURLEY .... Michael Gyngell
GEORGE SCOURIE .... Tom Hunsinger
WIBBLES .... Christopher Hurst
ALSATIAN FOGGERTY .... Mike Murray
CANARY ROBB .... Antony Simons
JANE .... Sarah Finch

INTRODUCTION

This adaptation of J.M. Barrie's play was prepared by us for the Royal Shakespeare Company in 1982. A brief explanation of some of the decisions we took in revising the text may be useful to anyone considering their own production of this version.

Embarking on our research for the play, we were intrigued to discover that there was no one single document called PETER PAN. What we found was a tantalizing number of different versions, all of them containing very agreeable surprises. We decided, therefore, to conflate a text from all the available variations. The resulting script was taken into rehearsal, where it underwent further emendation, and it finally found its way on to the Barbican stage. It is published for the first time in this edition.

J.M. Barrie wrote PETER PAN in 1903. He finally published it as a play in 1928. His reluctance to commit himself to a finished text was largely owing to the disappointment he felt in the productions of the play mounted before that date, and the limitations placed on his fantasy by the primitive theatrical techniques of the age. But emotionally too Barrie found it difficult to let his story go. Indeed so fascinated was he by his own creation that he could scarcely stop writing it! Like an inventive composer, he found that writing variations on a theme as good as PETER PAN could be an endless occupation.

We have used the 1928 play script as a basis for the present edition, but have also drawn from Barrie's "Notes for a Fairy Play," 1903; the original script of PETER PAN entitled ANON — A PLAY, 1903; the prompt script of the first production in 1904; the American version of 1905; the novel of 1911; and the film scenario which he wrote for Paramount in 1920 for Charlie Chaplin to play the part of Peter — a most imaginative piece of screen writing which, alas, never reached the screen. The final scene in which Peter meets the grown-up Wendy, is taken partly from the novel and partly from a long extra scene which Barrie wrote in 1907 entitled AN AFTER-THOUGHT, and which was performed once only, on 22nd February 1908.

We have included a lot of new material from this vast reservoir of discoveries, but have left out much more. There is no room, for instance, for the scene in which Peter and Wendy turn all the posh promenaders in Hyde Park into Harlequins and Columbines, and where we once again meet Hook, now a cruel schoolmaster. He is again swallowed by the Crocodile, who has crawled up out of the Serpentine, and he disappears down the animal's throat, pathetically begging Peter to be allowed to take a pack of cards with him! Another scene has "twenty beautiful mothers" showing up at the Darling house to claim their lost offspring, and being rejected by Peter for their bossiness, indifference or over-fastidiousness. There is an entirely unlikely marriage between Wendy and Tootles, and strangest of all, in one version of the final scene, Nana, twenty years on, has been stuffed and mounted as a rocking-horse dog for Wendy's daughter Jane. This macabre notion was, happily, rejected by Barrie almost as soon as he had written it!

We have made some significant alterations, the greatest of which is the introduction of a new character, the Storyteller, who is in fact the author himself. To a reader of the play, one of its most enjoyable ingredients is Barrie's unmistakable authorial tone. He tells the story of Peter Pan, partly through dialogue and partly by means of his inimitable stage directions. In a whimsical, ambiguous and ironical manner he speaks here as clearly to adults as he does to children. Moreover, many of the play's complicated conceits are only comprehensible if Barrie's commentary can be heard in parallel with the voices of his characters. This device also allows us to prepare our audience with some essential background history of the Darling family in a brief prologue, and to extend the narrative at the end of the play to include Barrie's heartbreaking and heartwarming conclusion to Peter and Wendy's story.

One of Barrie's most bitter disappointments was the quickly established tradition of having an actress play the part of Peter. He had wanted a real little boy to play the part but the laws of the land forbade children being on the stage after nine o'clock at night, so his wishes were confounded. He then tried to persuade his producer, Charles Frohmann, to cast Gerald du Maurier in the part, but he was overruled and the role was created by Nina Boucicault. Within a few years Barrie's wonderful fantasy had become what he most dreaded — a pantomime, as it is still most often played today. The problem remains. The part of Peter is, in fact, much too complex and emotionally challenging for a small child to perform successfully, but to allow a play about a boy and a girl to be acted out by two grown women is really most perverse. We solved the problem by casting all the children's roles with young adult actors and asking the audience to believe that they were children. Barrie instructs that "all the characters, whether grown ups, or babies, must wear a child's outlook on life as their only important adornment." It is a short step from this statement to requiring a group of twenty-year-old actors to become a group of ten-year-old lost boys, and requiring an audience to join in the conspiracy! And so they did. For three consecutive years at the Barbican theatre, audiences conspired to believe that an assortment of stage-scarred actors were really a band of innocent children. And so they always will if the parts are played well enough. Most actors, young and old, find a return to their childhood surprisingly easy, and if the actors make the journey with sufficient belief, the audience is sure to follow.

One small, but apparently important, detail has been omitted from the 1928 script. In the nursery in Act One, Peter refuses to let Wendy touch him, and Barrie adds, in a stage direction, "He is never touched by anyone in the play." This idea was not part of the author's original plan. It was added for Jean Forbes-Robertson's spiritual and Ariel-like performance in the late '20s. We have left it out because of its inconsistency both with Peter's character and with the action of the play. Peter is required to touch members of his tribe on numerous occasions, some of them quite essential for the story to unwind. More importantly, we felt that an audience should believe in Peter not as an airy sprite but as a thoroughly boyish little boy. There are fairies enough in the Never Land without Peter adding to their number. Tinker Bell herself is an extremely physical and female example of one, conceived by Barrie as "a girl exquisitely gowned in a skeleton leaf, cut low and square, through which her figure can be seen to best advantage. She was slightly inclined to embonpoint." We have included her actual dialogue in the script, drawn from Barrie's own texts and from inspired guesses. However, whether she is aurally represented by a tinkling bell or, as in our production, with the added help of an ingenious electronic device, her words should never be entirely audible, as it is only Peter, and her own fairy colleagues, who ever fully understand her language.

The Starkey/Smee front cloth scene between Acts Four and Five was written by Barrie in an awful hurry to cover a nasty scene change from the Never Land back to the Nursery. It isn't terribly good and is eminently cutable, but we needed it. If you can do without it, well done! But if you have a Never Land as complete and as beautiful as ours, and a Darling Home as perfect — both designed by our friend and colleague John Napier — you'll need the Starkey/Smee scene too!

Our single most important debt in the presentation of this edition is to Andrew Birkin, who first gave us access to all the source material, and guided us through it with an expert and a friendly hand. His remarkable television series THE LOST BOYS movingly documents the relationship between J.M. Barrie and the Llewellyn-Davies family, the tie which first inspired his creation of the play. The research done for this series also forms the basis of Andrew Birkin's book *The Lost Boys*, published by Constable in 1979. For anyone who seeks to understand the genesis of the Peter Pan myth and the tragic story behind it, this is essential reading.

Perhaps the most revealing comment Barrie ever made on the character of Peter was in a program note for the Paris production of 1908:

> "Of Peter himself you must make what
> you will. Perhaps he was a little boy
> who died young, and this is how the
> author conceived his subsequent adventures.
> Perhaps he was a boy who was
> never born at all — a boy whom some
> people longed for, but who never came.
> It may be that those people hear him
> at the window more clearly than
> children do."

This last remark was certainly, and most poignantly, true of Barrie himself and may go some way towards explaining his reluctance to publishing a final version of his child's adventures. We hope that the present edition remains faithful to the father's intentions and to the child's spirit, and that it will be as well appreciated by the lost parents of the Never Land as by their lost children.

Barrie's original dedication is included in this volume in full and it is, without question, to the five Llewellyn-Davies boys that the work owes its greatest inspiration. If we may be allowed our own dedication it is to the memory of our dear friend, Stephen Oliver, whose ravishingly beautiful and haunting score was one of the most memorable features of our production. Stephen was a composer of real genius, and a Peter Pan himself, who piped melodies of great sweetness all his life. Stephen's music, just like Peter's, will play on, and on, and on, till we wake up.

John Caird
Trevor Nunn

TO THE FIVE

A Dedication

Some disquieting confessions must be made in printing at last the play of PETER PAN; among them this, that I have no recollection of having written it. Of that, however, anon. What I want to do first is to give Peter to the Five without whom he never would have existed. I hope, my dear sirs, that in memory of what we have been to each other you will accept this dedication with your friend's love. The play of Peter is streaky with you still, though none may see this save ourselves. A score of Acts had to be left out, and you were in them all. We first brought Peter down, didn't we, with a blunt-headed arrow in Kensington Gardens? I seem to remember that we believed we had killed him, though he was only winded, and that after a spasm of exultation in our prowess the more soft-hearted among us wept and all of us thought of the police. There was not one of you who would not have sworn as an eye-witness to this occurrence; no doubt I was abetting, but you used to provide corroboration that was never given to you by me. As for myself, I suppose I always knew that I made Peter by rubbing the five of you violently together, as savages with two sticks produce a flame. That is all he is, the spark I got from you.

We had good sport of him before we clipped him small to make him fit the boards. Some of you were not born when the story began and yet were hefty figures before we saw that the game was up. Do you remember a garden at Burpham and the initiation there of No. 4 when he was six weeks old, and three of you grudged letting him in so young? Have you No. 3, forgotten the white violets at the Cistercian abbey in which we cassocked our first fairies (all little friends of St. Benedict), or your cry to the Gods, "Do I just kill one pirate all the time?" Do you remember Marooners' Hut in the haunted groves of Waverley, and the St. Bernard dog in a tiger's mask who so frequently attacked you, and the literary record of that summer, THE BOY CASTAWAYS, which is so much the best and the rarest of this author's works? What was it that made us eventually give to the public in the thin form of a play that which had been woven for ourselves alone? Alas, I know what it was, I was losing my grip. One by one as you swung monkey-wise from branch to branch in the wood of make-believe you reached the tree of knowledge. Sometimes you swung back into the wood, as the unthinking may at a cross-road take a familiar path that no longer leads to home; or you perched ostentatiously on its boughs to please me, pretending that you still belonged; soon you knew it only as the vanished wood, for it vanishes if one needs to look for it. A time came when I saw that No. 1, the most gallant of you all, ceased to believe that he was ploughing woods incarnadine and with an apologetic eye for me derided the lingering faith of No. 2; when even No. 3 questioned gloomily whether he did not really spend his nights in bed. There were still two who knew no better, but their day was dawning. In these circumstances, I suppose, was begun the writing of the play of Peter. That was a quarter of a century ago, and I clutch my brows in vain to remember whether it was a last desperate throw to retain the five of you for a little longer, or merely a cold decision to turn you into bread and butter.

This brings us back to my uncomfortable admission that I have no recollection of writing the play of PETER PAN, now being published for the first time so long after he made his bow upon the stage. You had played it until you tired of it, and tossed it in the air and gored it and left it derelict in the mud and went on your way singing other songs; and then I stole back and sewed some of the gory fragments together with a pen-nib. That is what must have happened, but I cannot remember doing it. I remember writing the story of PETER AND WENDY many years after the production of the play, but I might have cribbed that from some typed copy. I can haul back to mind the writing of almost every other as-say of mine, however forgotten by the pretty public; but this play of Peter, no. Even my beginning as an amateur playwright, that noble mouthful, BANDELERO THE BANDIT, I remember every detail of its composition in my school days at Dumfries. Not less vivid is my first little piece, produced by Mr. Toole. It was called IBSEN'S GHOST, and was a parody of the mightiest craftsman that ever wrote for our kind friends in front. To save the management the cost of typing I wrote out the "parts," after being told what parts were, and I can still recall my first words, spoken so plaintively by a now famous actress, — "To run away from my second husband just as I ran away from my first, it feels quite like old times." On the first night a man in the pit found IBSEN'S GHOST so diverting that he had to be removed in hysterics. After that no one seems to have thought of it at all. But what a man to carry about with one! How odd, too, that these trifles should adhere to the mind that cannot remember the long job of writing Peter. It does seem almost suspicious, especially as I have not the original manuscript of PETER PAN (except a few stray pages) with which to support my claim. I have indeed another manuscript, lately made, but that "proves nothing." I know not whether I lost that original manuscript or destroyed it or happily gave it away. I talk of dedicating the play to you, but how can I prove it is mine? How ought I to act if some other hand, who could also have made a copy, thinks it worth while to contest the cold rights? Cold they are to me now as that laughter of yours in which Peter came into being long before he was caught and written down. There is Peter still, but to me he lies sunk in the gay Black Lake.

Any one of you five brothers has a better claim to the authorship than most, and I would not fight you for it, but you should have launched your case long ago in the days when you most admired me, which were in the first year of the play, owing to a rumor's reaching you that my spoils were one-and-sixpence a night. This was untrue, but it did give me a standing among you. You watched for my next play with peeled eyes, not for entertainment but lest it contained some chance witticism of yours that could be challenged as collaboration; indeed I believe there still exists a legal document, full of the Aforesaid and Henceforward to be called Part-Author, in which for some such snatching I was tied down to pay No. 2 one halfpenny daily throughout the run of the piece.

During the rehearsals of Peter (and it is evidence in my favour that I was admitted to them) a depressed man in overalls, carrying a mug of tea or a paint-pot, used often to appear by my side in the shadowy stalls and say to me, "The gallery boys won't stand it." He then mysteriously faded away as if he were the theatre ghost. This hopelessness of his is what all dramatists are said to feel at such times, so perhaps he was the author. Again, a large number of children whom I have seen playing Peter in their homes with careless mastership, constantly putting in better words, could have thrown it off with ease. It was for such as they that after the first production I had to add something to the play at the request of parents (who thus showed that they thought me the responsible person) about no one being able to fly until the fairy dust had been blown on him; so many children having gone home and tried it from their beds and needed surgical attention.

Notwithstanding other possibilities, I think I wrote Peter and if so it must have been in the usual inky way. Some of it, I like to think, was done in that native place which is the dearest spot on earth to me, though my last heart-beats shall be with my beloved solitary London that was so hard to reach. I must have sat at a table with that great dog waiting for me to stop, not complaining, for he knew it was thus we made our living, but giving me a look when he found he was to be in the play, with his sex changed. In after years when the actor who was Nana had to go to the wars he first taught his wife how to take his place as the dog till he came back, and I am glad that I see nothing funny in this; it seems to me to belong to the play. I offer this obtuseness on my part as my first proof that I am the author.

Some say that we are different people at different periods of our lives, changing not through effort of will, which is a brave affair, but in the easy course of nature every ten years or so. I suppose this theory might explain my present trouble, but I don't hold with it; I think one remains the same person throughout, merely passing, as it were, in these lapses of time from one room to another, but all in the same house. If we unlock the rooms of the far past we can peer in and see ourselves, busily occupied in beginning to become you and me. Thus, if I am the author in question the way he is to go should already be showing in the occupant of my first compartment, at whom I now take the liberty to peep. Here he is at the age of seven or so with his fellow-conspirator Robb, both in glengarry bonnets. They are giving an entertainment in a tiny old washing-house that still stands. The charge for admission is preens, a bool, or a peerie (I taught you a good deal of Scotch, so possibly you can follow that), and apparently the culminating Act consists in our trying to put each other into the boiler, though some say that I also addressed the spell-bound audience. This washing-house is not only the theatre of my first play, but has a still closer connection with Peter. It is the original of the little house the Lost Boys built in the Never Land for Wendy, the chief difference being that it never wore John's tall hat as a chimney. If Robb had owned a lum hat I have no doubt that it would have been placed on the washing-house.

Here is that boy again some four years older, and the reading he is munching feverishly is about desert islands; he calls them wrecked islands. He buys his sanguinary tales surreptitiously in penny numbers. I see a change coming over him; he is blanching as he reads in the high-class magazine, CHATTERBOX, a fulmination against such literature, and sees that unless his greed for islands is quenched he is for ever lost. With gloaming he steals out of the house, his library bulging beneath his palpitating waistcoat. I follow like his shadow, as indeed I am, and watch him dig a hole in a field at Pathhead farm and bury his islands in it; it was ages ago, but I could walk straight to that hole in the field now and delve for the remains. I peep into the next compartment. There he is again, ten years older, an under-graduate now and craving to be a real explorer, one of those who do things instead of prating of them, but otherwise unaltered; he might be painted at twenty on top of a mast, in his hand a spy-glass through which he rakes the horizon for an elusive strand. I go from room to room, and he is now a man, real explora-tion abandoned (though only because no one would have him). Soon he is even concocting other plays, and quaking a little lest some low person counts how many islands there are in them. I note that with the years the islands grow more sin-ister, but it is only because he has now to write with the left hand, the right having given out; evidently one thinks more darkly down the left arm. Go to the keyhole of the compart-ment where he and I join up, and you may see us wondering whether they would stand one more island. This journey through the house may not convince any one that I wrote Peter, but it does suggest me as a likely person. I pause to ask myself whether I read CHATTERBOX again, suffered the old agony, and buried the manuscript of the play in a hole in a field.

Of course this is over-charged. Perhaps we do change; except a little something in us which is no larger than a mote in the eye, and that, like it, dances in front of us beguiling us all our days. I cannot cut the hair by which it hangs.

The strongest evidence that I am the author is to be found, I think, in a now melancholy volume, the aforementioned THE BOY CASTAWAYS; so you must excuse me for parading that work here. Officer of the Court, call THE BOY CAST-AWAYS. The witness steps forward and proves to be a book you remember well though you have not glanced at it these many years. I pulled it out of a bookcase just now not with-out difficulty, for its recent occupation has been to support the shelf above. I suppose, though I am uncertain, that it was

I and not you who hammered it into that place of utility. It is a little battered and bent after the manner of those who shoulder burdens, and ought (to our shame) to remind us of the witnesses who sometimes get an hour off from the cells to give evidence before his Lordship. I have said that it is the rarest of my printed works, as it must be, for the only edition was limited to two copies, of which one (there was always some devilry in any matter connected with Peter) instantly lost itself in a railway carriage. This is the survivor. The idlers in court may have assumed that it is a handwritten screed, and are impressed by its bulk. It is printed by Constable's (how handsomely you did us, dear Blaikie), it contains thirty-five illustrations and is bound in cloth with a picture stamped on the cover of the three eldest of you "setting out to be wrecked." This record is supposed to be edited by the youngest of the three, and I must have granted him that honour to make up for his being so often lifted bodily out of our adventures by his nurse, who kept breaking into them for the fell purpose of giving him a midday rest. No. 4 rested so much at this period that he was merely an honourary member of the band, waving his foot to you for luck when you set off with bow and arrow to shoot his dinner for him; and one may rummage the book in vain for any trace of No. 5. Here is the title page except that you are numbered instead of named —

THE BOY
CASTAWAYS
OF BLACK LAKE ISLAND
being a record of the Terrible
Adventures of Three Brothers
in the summer of 1901
faithfully set forth
by No. 3.

LONDON
Published by J.M. Barrie
in the Gloucester Road
1901

19

There is a long preface by No. 3 in which we gather your ages at this first flight. "No. 1 was eight and a month, No. 2 was approaching his seventh lustrum, and I was a good bit past four." Of his two elders, while commending their fearless dispositions, the editor complains that they wanted to do all the shooting and carried the whole equipment of arrows inside their shirts. He is attractively modest about himself. "Of No. 3 I prefer to say nothing, hoping that the tale as it is unwound will show that he was a boy of deeds rather than of words," a quality which he hints did not unduly protrude upon the brows of Nos. 1 and 2. His preface ends on a high note, "I should say that the work was in the first instance compiled as a record simply at which we could whet our memories, and that it is now published for No. 4's benefit. If it teaches him by example lessons in fortitude and manly endurance we shall consider that we were not wrecked in vain."

Published to whet your memories. Does it whet them? Do you hear once more, like some long-forgotten whistle beneath your window (Robb at dawn calling me to the fishing!) the not quite mortal blows that still echo in some of the chapter headings? — "Chapter II, No. 1 teaches Wilkinson (his master) a Stern Lesson — We Run Away to Sea. Chapter III, A Fearful Hurricane — Wreck of the "Anna Pink" — We Go Crazy from Want of Food — Proposal to eat No. 3 — Land Ahoy." Such are two chapters out of sixteen. Are these again your javelins cutting tunes in the blue haze of the pines; do you sweat as you scale the dreadful Valley of Rolling Stones; and cleanse your hands of pirate blood by scouring them carelessly in Mother Earth? Can you still make a fire (you could do it once, Mr. Seton-Thompson taught us in, surely an odd place, the Reform Club) by rubbing those sticks together? Was it the travail of hut-building that subsequently advised Peter to find a "home under the ground?" The bottle and mugs in that lurid picture, "Last night on the Island," seem to suggest that you had changed from Lost Boys into pirates, which was probably also a tendency of Peter's. Listen again to our stolen saw-mill, man's proudest invention; when he made the saw-mill he beat the birds for music in a wood.

The illustrations (full-paged) in THE BOY CASTAWAYS are all photographs taken by myself; some of them indeed of phenomena that had to be invented afterwards, for you were always off doing the wrong things when I pressed the button. I see that we combined instruction with amusement; perhaps we had given our kingly work to that effect. How otherwise account for such wording to the pictures as these: "It is undoubtedly," says No. 1 in a fir tree that is bearing unwonted fruit, recently tied to it, "the *Cocos nucifera,* for observe the slender columns supporting the crown of leaves which fall with a grace that no art can imitate." "Truly," continues No. 1 under the same tree in another forest as he leans upon his trusty gun, "though the perils of these happenings are great, yet would I rejoice to endure still greater privations to be thus rewarded by such wondrous studies of Nature." He is soon back to the practical, however, "recognising the Mango *(Magnifera indica)* by its lancet-shaped leaves and the cucumber-shaped fruit." No. 1 was certainly the right sort of voyager to be wrecked with, though if my memory fails me not, No. 2, to whom these strutting observations were addressed, sometimes protested because none of them was given to him. No. 3 being the author is in surprisingly few of the pictures, but this, you may remember was because the lady already darkly referred to used to pluck him from our midst for his siesta at 12 o'clock, which was the hour that best suited the camera. With a skill on which he has never been complimented the photographer sometimes got No. 3 nominally included in a wild-life picture when he was really in a humdrum house kicking on the sofa. Thus in a scene representing Nos. 1 and 2 sitting scowling outside the hut it is untruly written that they scowled because "their brother was within singing and playing on a barbaric instrument." The music, the unseen No. 3 is represented as saying (obviously forestalling No. 1), "is rude and to a cultured ear discordant, but the songs like those of

the Arabs are full of poetic imagery." He was perhaps allowed
to say this sulkily on the sofa.

Though THE BOY CASTAWAYS has sixteen chapter headings,
there is no other letterpress; an absence which possible pur-
chasers might complain of, though there are surely worse ways
of writing a book than this. These headings anticipate much
of the play of PETER PAN, but there were many incidents of
our Kensington Gardens days that never got into the book,
such as our Antarctic exploits when we reached the Pole in
advance of our friend Captain Scott and cut our initials on it
for him to find, a strange foreshadowing of what was really to
happen. In THE BOY CASTAWAYS Captain Hook has arrived
but is called Captain Swarthy, and he seems from the pictures
to have been a black man. This character, as you do not need
to be told, is held by those in the know to be autobiographi-
cal. You had many tussles with him (though you never, I
think, got his right arm) before you reached the terrible chapter (which might be taken from the play) entitled "We Board
the Pirate Ship at Dawn — A Rakish Craft — No. 1 Hew-
them-Down and No. 2 of the Red Hatchet — A Holocaust of
Pirates — Rescue of Peter." (Hullo, Peter rescued instead of
rescuing others? I know what that means and so do you, but
we are not going to give away all our secrets) The scene of
the Holocaust is the Black Lake (afterwards, when we let
women in, the Mermaids' Lagoon) The pirate captain's end
was not in the mouth of a Crocodile though we had Croco-
diles on the spot ("while No. 2 was removing the Crocodiles
from the stream No. 1 shot a few parrots, *Psittacidae,* for our
evening meal"). I think our captain had divers deaths owing
to unseemly competition among you, each wanting to slay him
single-handed. On a special occasion, such as when No. 3
pulled out the tooth himself, you gave the deed to him, but
took it from him while he rested. The only pictorial represen-
tation in the book of Swarthy's fate is in two parts. In one,
called briefly "We string him up." Nos. 1 and 2, stern as
Athos, are hauling him up a tree by a rope, his face snarling
as if it were a grinning mask (which indeed it was), and his

garments very like some of my own stuffed with bracken. The other, the same scene next day, is called "The Vultures had Picked him Clean," and tells its own tale.

The dog in THE BOY CASTAWAYS seems never to have been called Nana but was evidently in training for that post. He originally belonged to Swarthy (or to Captain Marryat?), and the first picture of him, lean, skulking, and hunched (how did I get that effect?), "patrolling the island" in that monster's interests, gives little indication of the domestic paragon he was to become. We lured him away to the better life, and there is, later, a touching picture, a clear forecast of the Darling nursery, entitled "We trained the dog to watch over us while we slept." In this he also is sleeping, in a position that is a careful copy of his charges; indeed any trouble we had with him was because, once he knew he was in the story, he thought his safest course was to imitate you in everything you did. How anxious he was to show that he understood the game, and more generous than you, he never pretended that he was the one who killed Captain Swarthy. I must not imply that he was entirely without initiative, for it was his own idea to bark warningly a minute or two before twelve o'clock as a signal to No. 3 that his keeper was probably on her way for him (Disappearance of No. 3); and he became so used to living in the world of Pretend that when we reached the hut of a morning he was often there waiting for us, looking, it is true, rather idiotic, but with a new bark he had invented which puzzled us until we decided that he was demanding the password. He was always willing to do any extra jobs, such as becoming the tiger in mask, and when after fierce engagement you carried home that mask in triumph, he joined in the procession proudly and never let on that the trophy had ever been part of him. Long afterwards he saw the play from a box in the theatre, and as familiar scenes were unrolled before his eyes I have never seen a dog so bothered. At one matinee we even let him for a moment take the place of the actor who played Nana, and I don't know that any members of the audience ever noticed the change, though he introduced some "business" that was new to them but old to you and me. Heigh-ho, I suspect that in this reminiscence I am mixing him up with his successor, for such a one there had to be, the loyal Newfoundland who, perhaps in the following year, applied, so to say, for the part by bringing hedgehogs to the hut in his mouth as offerings for our evening repasts. The head and coat of him were copied for the Nana of the play.

They do seem to be emerging out of our island, don't they, the little people of the play, all except that sly one, the chief figure, who draws farther and farther into the wood as we advance upon him? He so dislikes being tracked, as if there were something odd about him, that when he dies he means to get up and blow away the particle that will be his ashes.

Wendy has not yet appeared, but she has been trying to come ever since that loyal nurse cast the humorous shadow of woman upon the scene and made us feel that it might be fun to let in a disturbing element. Perhaps she would have bored her way in at last whether we wanted her or not. It may be that even Peter did not really bring her to the Never Land of his free will, but merely pretended to do so because she would not stay away. Even Tinker Bell had reached our island before we left it. It was one evening when we climbed the wood carrying No. 4 to show him what the trail was like by twilight. As our lanterns twinkled among the leaves No. 4 saw a twinkle stand still for a moment and he waved his foot gaily to it, thus creating Tink. It must not be thought, however, that there were any other sentimental passages between No. 4 and Tink; indeed, as he got to know her better he suspected her of frequenting the hut to see what we had been having for supper, and to partake of the same, and he pursued her with malignancy.

A safe but sometimes chilly way of recalling the past is to force open a crammed drawer. If you are searching for anything in particular you don't find it, but something falls out at the back that is often more interesting. It is in this way that I get my desultory reading, which includes a few stray leaves of the original manuscript of Peter that I have said I do possess, though even they, when returned to the drawer, are gone again, as if that touch of devilry lurked in them still. They show that in early days I hacked at and added to the play. In the drawer I find some scraps of Mr. Crook's delightful music, and other incomplete matter relating to Peter. Here is the reply of a boy whom I favoured with a seat in my box and injudiciously asked at the end what he had liked best. "What I think I liked best," he said, "was tearing up the programme and dropping the bits on people's heads." Thus am I often laid low. A copy of my favorite programme of the play is still in the drawer. In the first or second year of Peter, No. 4 could not attend through illness, so we took the play to his nursery, far away in the country, an array of vehicles almost as glorious as a travelling circus; the leading parts were played by the youngest children in the London company, and No. 4, aged five, looked on solemnly at the performance from his bed and never smiled once. That was my first and only appearance on the real stage, and this copy of the programme shows I was thought so meanly of as an actor that they printed my name in smaller letters than the others.

I have said little here of Nos. 4 and 5, and it is high time I had finished. They had a long summer day, and I turn round twice and now they are off to school. On Monday, as it seems, I was escorting No. 5 to a children's party and brushing his hair in the ante-room; and by Thursday he is placing me against the wall of an underground station and saying, "Now I am going to get the tickets; don't move till I come back for you or you'll lose yourself." No. 4 jumps from being astride my shoulders fishing, I knee-deep in the stream, to becoming, while still a schoolboy, the sternest of my literary critics. Anything he shook his head over I abandoned, and conceivably the world has thus been deprived of masterpieces. There was for instance an unfortunate little tragedy which I liked until I foolishly told No. 4 its subject, when he frowned and said he had better have a look at it. He read it, and then, patting me on the back, as only he and No. 1 could touch me, said, "You know you can't do this sort of thing." End of a tragedian. Sometimes, however, No. 4 liked my efforts, and I walked in the azure that day when he returned *Dear Brutus* to me with the comment "Not so bad." In earlier days, when he was ten, I offered him the manuscript of my book *Margaret Ogilvy*. "Oh, thanks," he said almost immediately, and added, "Of course my desk is awfully full." I reminded him that he could take out some of its more ridiculous contents. He said "I have read it already in the book." This I had not known, and I was secretly elated, but I said that people sometimes liked to preserve this kind of thing as a curiosity. He said "Oh" again. I said tartly that he was not compelled to take it if he didn't want it. He said "Of course I want it, but my desk —" Then he wriggled out of the room and came back in a few minutes dragging in No. 5 and announcing triumphantly, "No. 5 will have it."

The rebuffs I have got from all of you! They were especially crushing in those early days when one by one you came out of your belief in fairies and lowered on me as the deceiver. My grandest triumph, the best thing in the play of PETER PAN (though it is not in it) is that long after No. 4 had ceased to believe, I brought him back to the faith for at least two minutes. We were on our way in a boat to fish the Outer Hebrides (where we caught *Mary Rose*), and though it was a journey of days he wore his fishing basket on his back all the time, so as to be able to begin at once. His one pain was the absence of Johnny Mackay, for Johnny was the loved gillie of the previous summer who had taught him everything that is worth knowing (which is a matter of flies) but could not be with us this time as he would have had to cross and re-cross Scotland to reach us. As the boat drew near the Kyle of Lochalsh pier I told Nos. 4 and 5 it was such a famous wishing pier, that they had now but to wish and they should have. No. 5 believed at once and expressed a wish to meet himself (I afterwards found him on the pier searching faces confidently), but No. 4 thought it more of my untimely nonsense and doggedly declined to humor me. "Whom do you want to see most, No. 4?" "Of course I would like most to see Johnny Mackay." "Well, then, wish for him." "Oh, rot." "It can't do any harm to wish." Contemptuously he wished, and as the ropes were thrown on the pier he saw Johnny waiting for him, loaded with angling paraphernalia. I know no one less like a fairy than Johnny Mackay, but for two minutes No. 4 was quivering in another world than ours. When he came to he gave me a smile which meant that we understood each other, and thereafter neglected me for a month, being always with Johnny. As I have said, this episode is not in the play; so though I dedicate PETER PAN to you I keep the smile, with the few other broken fragments of immortality that have come my way.

J. M. Barrie

PETER PAN

PROLOGUE

Music. Darkness. A match is lit, and a light comes up on a slight man, impeccably attired in evening dress. He is lighting a pipe. He addresses the audience.

STORYTELLER.   Have you ever seen a map of a person's mind? Doctors sometimes draw maps of other parts of you, but catch them trying to draw a map of a child's mind, which is not only confused, but keeps going round all the time. If you ever did see a map like that, you would be looking at a map of the Never Land. There are zig-zag lines on it (just like your temperature on a card) and these are probably roads on the island — for the Never Land is always more or less an island, with astonishing splashes of colour here and there, *(Actors start to appear in the darkness around the Storyteller, like a herd of curious cattle.)* and coral reefs, and rakish looking craft in the offing, and savages, and lonely lairs, and gnomes who are mostly tailors, and princes with six elder brothers, and a hut fast going to decay, and one very small old lady with a hooked nose.

It would be an easy map if that were all, but there is also first day at school, religion, fathers, the round pond, needlework, murders, hangings, verbs that take the dative, chocolate pudding day, getting into braces, say ninety-nine, threepence for pulling out your tooth yourself, and so on; and either these are part of the island or they are another map showing through.

On these magic shores, children at play are forever beaching their coracles. We too have been there. We can still hear the sound of the surf, though we shall never land there any more.

All children grow up, except one. *(Peter appears at the back of the stage.)* Peter Pan ... the boy who wouldn't grow up. Let us tell the story of Peter Pan. *(The company of actors move D., allowing space behind them for the Darling house to arrive, when its cue comes, and they begin to act out the story.)* There never was a simpler, happier family than the Darling family. *(Mrs. Darling presents herself.)* Mrs. Darling was a lovely lady with a romantic mind and a sweet mocking mouth, which had one kiss on it that nobody could ever get. The way Mr. Darling won her was this. The many gentlemen who had been boys when she was a girl discovered simultaneously that they loved her, and they all ran to her house to propose to her, except Mr. Darling, *(Mr. Darling joins his wife.)* ...

MR. DARLING.   ... who took a cab and nipped in first.

STORYTELLER.   And so he got her.

MRS. DARLING.   He got all of her.

MR. DARLING.   Except that kiss.

STORYTELLER.   Mr. and Mrs. Darling had three children. *(The children join their parents.)*

WENDY.   Wendy came first.

JOHN.   And then John.

MICHAEL.   And then Michael.

MRS. DARLING.   Mrs. Darling loved to have everything just so,

STORYTELLER.   ... and Mr. Darling had a passion for being exactly like their neighbours,

MR. DARLING.   ... so, of course, they had to have a nurse for the children.

STORYTELLER.   But as they were so poor —

WENDY.   — owing to the amount of milk the children drank —

STORYTELLER.   — their nurse was a very large dog called Nana. *(Although this may shock the grandiose, the not exactly affluent will make allowances. The Darlings could not afford indeed to have a nurse, they could not afford indeed to have children; and now you are beginning to understand how they did it. Of course Nana has been trained by Mrs. Darling, but like all treasures she was born to it. In this play we shall see her chiefly inside the house, but she was just as exemplary outside, escorting the two elders to school with an umbrella in her mouth, for instance, and butting them back into line if they strayed.)*

THE DARLINGS.   Nana! Nana! Nana! *(Enter Nana knocking children over, and barking happily.)*

MRS. DARLING.   She proved to be quite a treasure.

STORYTELLER.   Their only other servant was Liza. *(Liza steps forward. She is so small that when she says she will never see ten again one can scarcely believe her.)* Such a midget she looked in her long skirt and maid's cap, ...

MRS. DARLING.   ... and somehow the Darlings had got into the way of calling her "the servants." *(Music, and the whole family dances.)*

STORYTELLER.   They all had lovely dances, and sometimes Liza was allowed to join in. The gaiety of those romps! And the gayest of all was Mrs. Darling, who would pirouette so wildly that all you could see of her was ... the kiss. There never was a simpler, happier family, until the coming of Peter Pan. *(The Darlings leave the stage.)* They lived at number 14 in a rather depressed street in Bloomsbury. *(We have a right to place the house where we will, and the reason Bloomsbury is chosen is that Mr. Roget once lived there. So did we in days when his thesaurus was our only companion in London; and we whom he has helped to wend our way through life have always wanted to pay him a little compliment. The Darlings therefore live in Bloomsbury.*

It is a corner house whose top window, the important one, looks upon a leafy square from which Peter used to fly up to it, to the delight of three children and, no doubt, the irritation of passersby. The street is still there, though the steaming sausage shop has gone; and apparently the same cards perch now as then over the doors, inviting homeless ones to come and stay with the hospitable inhabitants. Since the days of the Darlings, however, a lick of paint has been applied; and our corner house in particular, which has swallowed its neighbour, blooms with an awful freshness as if the colours had been discharged upon it with a hose. Its card now says "no children," meaning maybe that the goings-on of Wendy and her brothers have given the house a bad name. As for ourselves we have not been in it since we went back to reclaim our old thesaurus.)

This is what we call the Darling house, but you may dump it down anywhere you like, and if you think it was your house you are very probably right. it wanders about London looking for anybody in need of it. *(The rest of the company have been slowly leaving the stage as the house, or that part of it that is the nursery, begins to appear ...)*

END OF PROLOGUE

ACT ONE

THE NURSERY

STORYTELLER. *(Walking around the room he is describing.)*
The scene of our opening act is the night-nursery of the Darling family, a shabby little room if Mrs. Darling had not made it the hub of creation by her certainty that such it was, and adorned it to match with a loving heart and all the scrapings of her purse. *(The door on the right leads into the day nursery, which she has no right to have, but she made it herself with nails in her mouth and a paste-pot in her hand. This is the door the children will come in by. There are three beds and a large dog-kennel; two of these beds, with the kennel, being on the left and the other on the right.)* The coverlets of the beds are made out of her wedding gown. *(Over each bed is a china house, the size of a linnet's nest, containing a night-light.)* Supporting the mantle shelf are two soldiers, home-made, begun by Mr. Darling, finished by Mrs. Darling, repainted (unfortunately) by John Darling. *(On the fire-guard hang incomplete parts of children's night attire. The door on the left leads to the bathroom. In the center is the window, which is at present ever so staid and respectable, but half an hour hence will be able to tell a very strange tale to the police.)* It was the spring of the year. Wendy was already nearly twelve by now, John was ten and Michael was still so small that he spent most of his time doing idiotic things with a teddy-bear. The only occupant of the room at present is Nana. The cuckoo-clock strikes six ... *(As the clock starts to strike the Storyteller quietly leaves the stage, and Nana springs into life. This first moment in the play is tremendously important, for if the actor playing Nana does not spring properly we are undone. She will probably be played by a boy, if one clever enough can be found, and must never be on two legs except on those rare occasions when an ordinary nurse would be on four. The Nana must go about all her duties in a most ordinary manner so that you know in your bones that she performs them*

just so every evening at six; naturalness must be her passion; indeed it should be the aim of everyone in the play, for which she is now setting the pace. All the characters, whether grown-ups or babes, must wear a child's outlook on life as their only important adornment. If they cannot help being funny they are begged to go away. A good motto for all would be "the little less, and how much it is." Nana, making much use of her mouth, "turns down" the beds, and carries the various articles on the fire-guard across to them. Michael enters and Nana barks at him.)

MICHAEL. *(Obstreperous.)* I won't go to bed, I won't, I won't. Nana, it isn't six o'clock yet. Two minutes more, please, one minute more? Nana, I won't be bathed, I tell you I will not be bathed. Well, I won't have my head washed! *(Here the bathroom door closes on them, and Mrs. Darling, who has perhaps heard his cry, enters the nursery. As she is going out to dinner tonight she is already wearing her evening gown because she knows her children like to see her in it. It is a delicious confection made by herself out of nothing and other people's mistakes. She does not often go out to dinner, preferring when the children are in bed to sit beside them tidying up their minds, just as if they were drawers. If Wendy and the boys could keep awake they might just see her repacking into their proper places the many articles of the mind that have strayed during the day, lingering humorously over some of their contents, wondering where on earth they picked this thing up, making discoveries sweet and not so sweet, pressing this to her cheek and hurriedly stowing that out of sight. When they wake in the morning the naughtinesses with which they went to bed are not, alas, blown away, but they are placed at the bottom of the drawer; and on the top, beautifully aired, are their prettier thoughts ready for the new day. As she enters the room she is startled to see a strange little face outside the window and a hand groping as if it wanted to come in.)*

MRS. DARLING. Who are you? *(The unknown disappears; she hurries to the window.)* No one there. And yet I feel sure I saw a face. My children! *(She throws open the bathroom door and Michael's head appears gaily over the bath. He splashes; she throws kisses to him and closes the door.)* Wendy! John! *(Reassuring answers from the day nursery. She sits down, relieved, on Wendy's bed; and Wendy and John come in, looking their smallest size, as children*

tend to do to a mother suddenly in fear for them.)
JOHN.   *(Historionically.)* We are doing an act; we are playing at being you and father. *(He imitates the only father who has come under his special notice.)* A little less noise there.
WENDY.   Now let us pretend we have a baby.
JOHN.   I am happy to inform you, Mrs. Darling, that you are now a mother. *(Wendy gives way to ecstasy.)* You have missed the chief thing; you haven't asked, 'boy or girl?'
WENDY.   I am so glad to have one at all, I don't care which it is.
JOHN.   *(Crushingly.)* That is just the difference between gentlemen and ladies. Now you tell me.
WENDY.   I am happy to acquaint you, Mr. Darling, you are now a father.
JOHN.   Boy or girl?
WENDY.   *(Presenting herself.)* Girl.
JOHN.   Tsk.
WENDY.   You horrid.
JOHN.   Go on.
WENDY.   I am happy to acquaint you, Mr. Darling, you are again a father.
JOHN.   Boy or girl?
WENDY.   Boy. *(John beams.)* Mummy, it's hateful of him. *(Michael emerges from the bathroom in John's old pajamas and giving his face a last wipe with the towel.)*
MICHAEL.   *(Expanding.)* Now, John, have me.
JOHN.   We don't want any more.
MICHAEL.   *(Contracting.)* Am I not to be born at all?
JOHN.   Two is enough.
MICHAEL.   *(Wheedling.)* Come, John; boy, John. *(Appalled.)* Nobody wants me!
MRS. DARLING.   I do.
MICHAEL.   *(With a glimmer of hope.)* Boy or girl?
MRS. DARLING.   *(With one of those happy thoughts of hers.)* Boy. *(Triumph of Michael; discomfiture of John. Mr. Darling arrives, in no mood unfortunately to gloat over this domestic scene. He is really a good man as breadwinners go and it is hard luck for him to be propelled into the room now, when if we had brought him in a*

few minutes earlier or later he might have made a fairer impression. In the city where he sits on a stool all day, as fixed as a postage stamp, he is so like all the others on stools that you recognize him not by his face but by his stool, but at home the way to gratify him is to say that he has a distinct personality. He is very conscientious, and in the days when Mrs. Darling gave up keeping the house books correctly and drew pictures instead [which he called her guesses] he did all the totting up for her, holding her hand while he calculated whether they could have Wendy or not, and coming down on the right side. It is with regret, therefore, that we introduce him as a tornado, rushing into the nursery in evening dress, but without his coat, and brandishing in his hand a recalcitrant white tie.)

MR. DARLING. *(Implying that he has searched for her everywhere and that the nursery is a strange place to find her.)* Oh, here you are, Mary.

MRS. DARLING. *(Knowing at once what is the matter.)* What is the matter, George dear?

MR. DARLING. *(As if the word were monstrous.)* Matter! The matter is that I am a desperate man! This tie, it will not tie. *(He waxes sarcastic.)* Not round my neck. Round the bed-post, oh yes; twenty times have I made it up round the bed-post, but round my neck oh dear no; begs to be excused.

MICHAEL. *(In a joyous transport.)* Say it again, father, say it again!

MR. DARLING. *(Witheringly.)* Thank you. *(Goaded by a suspiciously crooked smile on Mrs. Darling's face.)* I warn you, Mary, that unless this tie is round my neck we don't go out to dinner to-night, and if I don't go out to dinner to-night, I never go to the office again, and if I don't go to the office again you and I starve, and our children will be thrown into the streets. *(The children blanch as they grasp the gravity of the situation.)*

MRS. DARLING. Let me try, dear. *(In a terrible silence their progeny cluster round them. Will she succeed? Their fate depends on it. She fails — no, she succeeds. In another moment they are wildly gay, romping round the room on each other's shoulders. Father is an even better horse than mother. Michael is dropped upon his bed, Wendy retires to prepare for hers, John runs from Nana, who has re-*

appeared with the bath towel.)

JOHN. *(Rebellious.)* I won't be bathed. You needn't think it.

MR. DARLING. *(In the grand manner.)* Go and be bathed at once, sir. *(With bent head John follows Nana into the bathroom. Mr. Darling swells.)*

MICHAEL. *(As he is put between the sheets.)* Mother, how did you get to know me?

MR. DARLING. A little less noise there.

MICHAEL. *(Growing solemn.)* At what time was I born, mother?

MRS. DARLING. At two o'clock in the night-time, dearest.

MICHAEL. Oh, mother, I hope I didn't wake you.

MRS. DARLING. They are rather sweet, don't you think, George?

MR. DARLING. *(Doting.)* There is not their equal on earth, and they are ours, ours! *(Unfortunately Nana has come in from the bathroom for a sponge and she collides with his trousers, the first pair he has ever had with braid on them.)* Mary, it is too bad; just look at this; covered with hairs. Clumsy, clumsy! *(Nana goes, a drooping figure.)*

MRS. DARLING. Let me brush you, dear. *(Once more she is successful. They are now by the fire, and Michael is in bed doing idiotic things with a teddy bear.)*

MR. DARLING. *(Depressed.)* I sometimes think, Mary, that it is a mistake to have a dog for a nurse.

MRS. DARLING. George, Nana is a treasure.

MR. DARLING. No doubt; but I have an uneasy feeling at times that she looks upon the children as puppies.

MRS. DARLING. *(Rather faintly.)* Oh no, dear one, I am sure she knows they have souls.

MR. DARLING. *(Profoundly.)* I wonder, I wonder.

MRS. DARLING. *(The opportunity has come for her to tell him of something that is on her mind.)* George, we must keep Nana. *(Her seriousness impresses him.)* When I came into this room to-night I saw a face at the window.

MR. DARLING. *(Incredulous.)* A face at the window, three floors up? Pooh!

MRS. DARLING. It was the face of a little boy; he was trying to get in.

MR. DARLING. Impossible! You can't be well, Mary. How many fingers am I holding up?

MRS. DARLING. Five.

MR. DARLING. How many now?

MRS. DARLING. One.

MR. DARLING. You seem to be all right.

MRS. DARLING. George, this is not the first time I have seen that boy.

MR. DARLING. *(Beginning to think that this may be a man's job.)* Oho!

MRS. DARLING. *(Making sure that Michael does not hear.)* The first time was a week ago. It was Nana's night out, and I had been drowsing here by the fire when suddenly I felt a draught, as if the window were open. I looked round and I saw that boy — in the room.

MR. DARLING. In the room?

MRS. DARLING. I screamed. The boy leapt through the window and slammed it behind him. I rushed down into the street to look for his little body on the pavement, and there was nothing there. I thought I must have dreamed it but when I returned to the nursery there on the floor lay his shadow. He had shut the window so quickly he had cut it clean off.

MR. DARLING. *(Heavily.)* Mary, Mary, why didn't you keep that shadow?

MRS. DARLING. *(Scoring.)* I did. I rolled it up, George; and here it is. *(She produces it from a drawer. They unroll and examine the flimsy thing, which is not more material than a puff of smoke, and if let go would probably float into the ceiling without discolouring it. Yet it has human shape. As they nod their heads over it they present the most satisfying picture on earth, two happy parents conspiring cozily by the fire for the good of their children.)*

MR. DARLING. It is nobody I know, but he does look a scoundrel.

MRS. DARLING. I think he comes back to get his shadow, George.

MR. DARLING. *(Meaning that the miscreant now has a father to deal with.)* There is money in this, my love. I shall take it to the British Museum tomorrow and have it priced. *(The shadow is rolled up and replaced in the drawer.)*

MRS. DARLING.   *(Like a guilty person.)* George, I have not told you all; I am afraid to.

MR. DARLING.   *(Who knows exactly the right moment to treat a woman as a beloved child.)* Cowardy, cowardy custard.

MRS. DARLING.   No, I'm not.

MR. DARLING.   Oh yes, you are.

MRS. DARLING.   George, I'm not.

MR. DARLING.   Then why not tell?

MRS. DARLING.   *(Thus cleverly soothed she goes on.)* The boy was not alone that first time. He was accompanied by — I don't know how to describe it; by a ball of light, not as big as my fist, but it darted about the room like a living thing.

MR. DARLING.   *(Though open-minded.)* That is very unusual. It escaped with the boy?

MRS. DARLING.   Yes. *(Sliding her hand into his.)* George, what can all this mean?

MR. DARLING.   *(Ever ready.)* What indeed? *(This intimate scene is broken by the return of Nana with a bottle in her mouth.)*

MRS. DARLING.   *(At once dissembling.)* What is that Nana? Ah, of course; Michael, it is your medicine.

MICHAEL.   *(Promptly.)* Won't take it.

MR. DARLING.   *(Recalling his youth.)* Be a man, Michael.

MICHAEL.   Won't.

MRS. DARLING.   *(Weakly.)* I'll get you a lovely chocky to take after it. *(She leaves the room, although her husband calls after her.)*

MR. DARLING.   Mary, don't pamper him. When I was your age, Michael, I took medicine without a murmur. I said "Thank you, kind parents, for giving me bottles to make me well." *(Wendy, who has appeared in her night-gown, hears this and believes.)*

WENDY.   That medicine you sometimes take is much nastier, isn't it, father?

MR. DARLING.   *(Valuing her support.)* Ever so much nastier. And as an example to you, Michael, I would take it now

39

(Thankfully.) if I hadn't lost the bottle.

WENDY.   *(Always glad to be of service.)* I know where it is, father. I'll fetch it. *(She is gone before he can stop her. He turns for help to John, who has come from the bathroom attired for bed.)*

MR. DARLING.   John, it is the most beastly stuff. It is that sticky sweet kind.

JOHN.   *(Who is perhaps still playing at parents.)* Never mind, father, it will soon be over. *(A spasm of ill-will to John cuts through Mr. Darling, and is gone. Wendy returns, Panting.)*

WENDY.   Here it is, father; I have been as quick as I could.

MR. DARLING.   *(With a sarcasm that is completely thrown away on her.)* You have been wonderfully quick, precious quick! *(He is now at the foot of Michael's bed, Nana is by its side, holding the medicine spoon insinuatingly in her mouth.)*

WENDY.   *(Proudly, as she pours out Mr. Darling's medicine.)* Michael, now you will see how father takes it.

MR. DARLING.   *(Hedging.)* Michael first.

MICHAEL.   *(Full of unworthy suspicions.)* Father first.

MR. DARLING.   It will make me sick, you know.

JOHN.   *(Lightly.)* Come on, father.

MR. DARLING.   Hold your tongue, sir.

WENDY.   *(Disturbed.)* I thought you took it quite easily, father, saying "Thank you, kind parents, for —"

MR. DARLING.   That is not the point; the point is that there is more in my glass than in Michael's spoon. It isn't fair, I swear though it were with my last breath, it is not fair.

MICHAEL.   *(Coldly.)* Father, I'm waiting.

MR. DARLING.   It's all very well to say you are waiting; so am I waiting.

MICHAEL.   Father's a cowardy custard.

MR. DARLING.   So are you a cowardy custard. *(They are now glaring at each other.)*

MICHAEL.   I am not frightened.

MR. DARLING.   Neither am I frightened.

MICHAEL.   Well, then, take it.

MR. DARLING.   Well then, you take it.

WENDY.   *(Butting in again.)* Why not take it at the same time?

MR. DARLING. *(Haughtily.)* Certainly. Are you ready, Michael?

WENDY. *(As nothing has happened.)* One – two – three. *(Michael partakes, but Mr. Darling resorts to hanky-panky.)*

JOHN. Father hasn't taken his! *(Michael howls.)*

WENDY. *(Inexpressibly pained.)* Oh father!

MR. DARLING. *(Who has been hiding the glass behind him.)* What do you mean by "Oh father?" I meant to take it but I missed it. Michael, stop that row! *(Nana shakes her head sadly over him, and goes into the bathroom. They are all looking as if they did not admire him, and nothing so dashes a temperamental man.)* I say, I have just thought of a splendid joke. *(They brighten.)* I shall pour my medicine into Nana's bowl and she will drink it thinking it is milk! *(The pleasantry does not appeal, but he prepares the joke, listening for appreciation.)*

WENDY. Poor darling Nana!

MR. DARLING. You silly little things; I am ashamed of you. *(They steal to their beds as Mrs. Darling returns with the chocolate followed by Liza, who proceeds to collect the hot-water bottles from the children's beds.)*

MRS. DARLING. Well, is it all over?

MICHAEL. Father didn't — *(Father glares.)*

MR. DARLING. All over, dear, quite satisfactorily. *(Nana comes back.)* Nana, good dog, good girl; I have put a little milk into your bowl. *(The bowl is C. and Nana begins to lap, only begins. She retreats into the kennel.)*

MRS. DARLING. What is the matter, Nana?

MR. DARLING. *(Uneasily.)* Nothing, nothing.

MRS. DARLING. *(Smelling the bowl.)* George, it is your medicine! *(The children break into lamentation. He gives his wife an imploring look; he is begging for one smile, but does not get it. In consequence he goes from bad to worse.)*

MR. DARLING. It was only a joke. Much good my wearing myself to the bone trying to be funny in this house.

WENDY. *(On her knees by the kennel.)* Father, Nana is crying.

MR. DARLING. Coddle her; nobody coddles me. Oh dear no. I am only the bread-winner, why should I be coddled? Why, why, why?

MRS. DARLING.   George, not so loud; the servants will hear you. *(Liza leaves the room with an armful of hot-water-bottles, and a discreet sniff in the direction of Mr. Darling.)*

MR. DARLING.   *(Defiant.)* Let them hear me; bring in the whole world. *(The desperate man, who has not been in fresh air for days, has now lost all self-control.)* I refuse to allow that dog to lord it in my nursery for one hour longer. *(Nana supplicates him.)* In vain, in vain, the proper place for you is the yard, and there you go to be tied up this instant. *(Nana again retreats into the kennel, and the children add their prayers to hers.)*

MRS. DARLING.   *(Who knows how contrite he will be for this presently.)* George, remember what I told you about that boy.

MR. DARLING.   Am I master in this house or is she? *(To Nana fiercely.)* Come along. *(He thunders at her, but she indicates that she has reasons not worth troubling him with for remaining where she is. He resorts to a false bonhomie.)* There, there, did she think he was angry with her, poor Nana? *(She wriggles a response in the affirmative.)* Good Nana, pretty Nana. *(She has seldom been called pretty, and it has the old effect. She plays rub-a-dub with her paws, which is how a dog blushes.)* She will come to her kind master, won't she? Won't she? *(She advances, retreats, waggles her head, her tail, and eventually goes to him. He seizes her collar in an iron grip and amid the cries of his progeny drags her from the room. They listen, for her remonstrances are not inaudible.)*

MRS. DARLING.   Be brave, my dears.

WENDY.   He is chaining Nana up! *(This unfortunately is what he is doing, though we cannot see him. Let us hope that he then retires to his study, looks up the word "temper" in his thesaurus, and under the influence of those benign pages becomes a better man. In the meantime the children have been put to bed in unwonted silence and Mrs. Darling tucks them in.)*

JOHN.   *(As the barking below goes on.)* She is awfully unhappy.

WENDY.   That is not Nana's unhappy bark. That is her bark when she smells danger.

MRS. DARLING.   *(Remembering that boy.)* Danger! Are you sure, Wendy?

WENDY.   *(The one of the family, for there is one in every family, who can be trusted to know or not to know.)* Oh yes. *(Her mother*

looks this way and that from the window.)
JOHN.   Is there anything there?
MRS. DARLING.   All quiet and still. Oh, how I wish I was not going out to dinner to-night.
MICHAEL.   Can anything harm us, mother, after the night-lights are lit?
MRS. DARLING.   Nothing, precious. They are the eyes a mother leaves behind her to guard her children. *(Nevertheless we may be sure she means to tell Liza, the little maid, to look in on them frequently till she comes home. She goes from bed to bed, after her custom, lighting the night lights and crooning a lullaby.)*
MICHAEL.   *(Drowsily.)* Mother I'm glad of you.
MRS. DARLING.   *(With a last look round, her hand on the switch.)* Dear night-lights that protect my sleeping babes, burn clear and steadfast tonight. *(The nursery darkens and she is gone, intentionally leaving the door ajar. Something uncanny is going to happen, we expect, for a quiver has passed through the room, just sufficient to touch the night-lights. They blink three times one after the other and go out, precisely as the children [whom familiarity has made them resemble] fall asleep. There is another light in the room now, no larger than Mrs. Darling's fist and in the time we have taken to say this, it has been into the drawers and wardrobe and searched pockets, as it darts about looking for a certain shadow. Then the window is blown open, probably by the smallest and therefore most mischievous star, and Peter Pan flies into the room. In so far as he is dressed at all, it is in autumn leaves and cobwebs.)*
PETER.   *(In a whisper.)* Tinker Bell, Tink, where are you? *(A jug lights up.)*
TINK.   *(The answer comes as of a tinkle of bells; it is the fairy language. Peter can speak it, but it bores him.)* I'm in here.
PETER.   Oh, do come out of that jug. *(Tink flashes hither and thither.)* Do you know where they put it?
TINK.   In the big box.
PETER.   Which big box?
TINK.   Over here.
PETER.   This one?
TINK.   Yes.
PETER.   But which drawer?

TINK. I'll show you if you like.

PETER. Yes, do show me. *(Tink pops into the drawer where the shadow is, but before Peter can reach it, Wendy moves in her sleep. Startled, Peter slips through the door into the bathroom for a moment, but reappears at once as Wendy has not waked. [A subtle adjustment has been made to his costume, but we don't notice it at all.] He crosses to the drawer and scatters its contents to the floor, as kings on their wedding day toss ha'pence to the crowd. In his joy at finding his shadow he forgets that he has shut up Tink in the drawer. He sits on the floor with the shadow, confident that he and it will join like drops of water. Then he tries to stick it on with soap from the bathroom, and this failing also, he subsides dejectedly on the floor. This wakens Wendy, who sits up, and is pleasantly interested to see a stranger.)*

WENDY. *(Courteously.)* Boy, why are you crying? *(He jumps up, and crossing to the foot of the bed bows to her in the fairy way. Wendy, impressed, bows to him from the bed.)*

PETER. What is your name?

WENDY. *(Well satisfied.)* Wendy Moira Angela Darling. What is yours?

PETER. *(Finding it lamentably brief.)* Peter Pan.

WENDY. Is that all?

PETER. *(Biting his lip.)* Yes.

WENDY. *(Politely.)* I am so sorry.

PETER. It doesn't matter.

WENDY. Where do you live?

PETER. Second on the right and then straight on till morning.

WENDY. What a funny address!

PETER. No, it isn't.

WENDY. I mean, is that what they put on the letters?

PETER. Don't get any letters.

WENDY. But your mother gets letters?

PETER. Don't have a mother.

WENDY. Peter! *(She leaps out of bed to put her arms round him, but he draws back.)* No wonder you were crying.

PETER. I wasn't crying about my mother. I was crying because I can't get my shadow to stick on. Anyway I wasn't crying.

WENDY.   It has come off! How awful. *(Looking at the spot where he had lain.)* Peter, you have been trying to stick it on with soap!

PETER.   *(Snappily.)* Well, then?

WENDY.   It must be sewn on.

PETER.   What is "sewn?"

WENDY.   You are dreadfully ignorant.

PETER.   No, I'm not.

WENDY.   I will sew it on for you my little man. Stand still. I dare say it will hurt a little.

PETER.   *(A recent remark of hers rankling.)* I never cry. *(She seems to sew the shadow to his heels. He bears the pain, and then tests the combination, but the flimsy thing drags uselessly behind him.)* It isn't quite itself yet.

WENDY.   Perhaps I should have ironed it.

PETER.   Perhaps it's dead.

WENDY.   I think we need a little more light. *(She touches something and to his astonishment the room is illuminated. The shadow awakes and is glad to be back with him as he is to have it. He and his shadow dance together. He is showing off now. He crows like a cock. He would fly in order to impress Wendy further if he knew that there is anything unusual in that.)*

PETER.   Wendy, look, look; oh the cleverness of me!

WENDY.   You conceit; of course I did nothing!

PETER.   You did a little.

WENDY.   *(Wounded.)* A little! If I am no use I can at least withdraw. *(With one haughty leap she is again in bed with the sheet over her face. Popping onto the end of the bed the artful one appeals.)*

PETER.   Wendy, don't withdraw. I can't help crowing, Wendy, when I'm pleased with myself. Wendy, one girl is worth more than twenty boys.

WENDY.   *(Peeping over the sheet.)* You really think so, Peter?

PETER.   Yes, I do.

WENDY.   I think it's perfectly sweet of you, and I shall get up again. *(They sit together on the side of the bed.)* I shall give you a kiss if you like.

PETER.   Thank you. *(He holds out his hand.)*

WENDY. (Aghast.) Don't you know what a kiss is?

PETER. I shall know when you give it me. (Not to hurt his feelings, she gives him her thimble.) Now shall I give you a kiss?

WENDY. (Primly.) If you please. (He pulls an acorn button off his person and bestows it on her. She is shocked but considerate.) I will wear it on this chain round my neck. Peter, how old are you?

PETER. (Blithely.) I don't know, but quite young, Wendy. I ran away the day I was born.

WENDY. Ran away, why?

PETER. Because I heard father and mother talking of what I was to be when I became a man. Wendy, I want always to be a little boy and to have fun; so I ran away to Kensington Gardens and lived a long time among the fairies.

WENDY. (With great eyes.) You know fairies, Peter!

PETER. (Surprised that this should be a recommendation.) Yes, but they are nearly all dead now. (Baldly.) You see, Wendy, when the first baby laughed for the first time, the laugh broke into a thousand pieces, and they all went skipping about, and that was the beginning of fairies. And now when every new baby is born its first laugh becomes a fairy. So there ought to be a fairy for every boy or girl.

WENDY. (Breathlessly.) Ought to be? Isn't there?

PETER. Oh no. Children know such a lot now. Soon they don't believe in fairies, and every time a child says "I don't believe in fairies" there is a fairy somewhere that falls down dead. (Heartlessly.) They just crumple up.

WENDY. Poor things!

PETER. (To whom this statement recalls a forgotten friend.) I can't think where she has gone. Tinker Bell, Tink, where are you?

WENDY. (Thrilling.) Peter, you don't mean to tell me that there is a fairy in this room!

PETER. (Flitting about in search.) She came in with me. You don't hear anything, do you?

WENDY. I hear — the only sound I hear is like a tinkle of bells.

PETER. That is the fairy language. I hear it too.

WENDY.   It seems to come from over there.

PETER.   *(With shameless glee.)* Wendy, I believe I shut her up in that drawer! *(He releases Tink, who darts about in a fury using language it is perhaps as well we can't understand.)* You needn't say that; I'm very sorry, but how could I know you were in the drawer?

WENDY.   *(Her eyes dancing in pursuit of the delicious creature.)* Oh Peter, if only she would stand still and let me see her!

PETER.   *(Indifferently.)* They hardly ever stand still. *(To show that she can do even this Tink passes between two ticks of the cuckoo clock.)*

WENDY.   I see her, the lovely! Where is she now?

PETER.   She is behind the clock. Tink, this lady wishes you were her fairy. *(The answer comes immediately.)*

WENDY.   What does she say?

PETER.   She is not very polite. She says you are a great ugly girl, and that she is my fairy. You know, Tink, you can't be my fairy because I am a gentleman and you are a lady. *(Tink replies.)*

WENDY.   What did she say?

PETER.   She said "You silly ass." She is quite a common girl, you know. She is called Tinker Bell because she mends the fairy pots and kettles.

WENDY.   Where do you live now?

PETER.   With the lost boys.

WENDY.   Who are they?

PETER.   They are the children who fall out of their prams when the nurse is looking the other way. If they are not claimed in seven days they are sent away to the Never Land. I'm captain.

WENDY.   What fun it must be.

PETER.   *(Craftily.)* Yes, but we are rather lonely. You see, Wendy, we have no female companionship.

WENDY.   Are none of the other children girls?

PETER.   Oh no; girls, you know, are much too clever to fall out of their prams.

WENDY.   Peter, it is perfectly lovely the way you talk about girls. John there just despises us. *(Peter, for the first time, has a good look at John. He then neatly tumbles him out of bed.)* You wicked! You are not captain here. *(She bends over her brother who is prone on the floor.)* After all he hasn't wakened, and you meant to be kind. *(Having done her duty she forgets John, who blissfully sleeps on.)* Peter, you may give me a kiss.

PETER.   *(Cynically.)* I thought you would want it back. *(He offers her the thimble.)*

WENDY.   *(Artfully.)* Oh dear, I didn't mean a kiss, Peter, I meant a thimble.

PETER.   *(Only half placated.)* What is that?

WENDY.   It is like this. *(She kisses him.)*

PETER.   *(Satisfied.)* Now shall I give you a thimble?

WENDY.   If you please. *(Before he can even draw near she screams.)*

PETER.   What is it?

WENDY.   It was exactly as if someone were pulling my hair.

PETER.   That must have been Tink. I never knew her so naughty before. *(Tink speaks. She is in the jug again.)*

WENDY.   What does she say?

PETER.   She says she will do that every time I give you a thimble.

WENDY.   But why?

PETER.   *(Equally nonplused.)* Why, Tink? *(He has to translate the answer.)* She said "You silly ass" again.

WENDY.   She is very impertinent. *(They are now sitting on the floor.)* Peter, why did you come to our nursery window?

PETER.   To try to hear stories. None of us knows any stories.

WENDY.   How perfectly awful!

PETER.   That's why swallows build in the eaves of houses. To listen to the stories. Wendy, your mother was telling you such a lovely story.

WENDY.   Which story was it?

PETER.   About the prince, and he couldn't find the lady who wore the glass slipper.

WENDY.   That was Cinderella. Peter, he found her and they were happy ever after.

PETER.   I am glad. *(They have worked their way along the floor close to each other, but now he jumps up.)*
WENDY.   Peter, where are you going?
PETER.   *(Already on his way to the window.)* To tell the other boys.
WENDY.   Don't go, Peter. I know lots of stories. The stories I could tell to the boys!
PETER.   *(Gleaming.)* Come with me then. We'll fly.
WENDY.   Fly? You can fly! *(How he would like to rip those stories out of her; he is dangerous now.)*
PETER.   Yes.
WENDY.   Oh dear, I mustn't. Think of mother.
PETER.   You shall! You shall! *(Seizes her.)*
WENDY.   Let go, Peter Pan. Besides, I can't fly.
PETER.   I'll teach you.
WENDY.   But I won't go away with you.
PETER.   You won't be able to help it —
WENDY.   Then I won't learn.
PETER.   I'll teach you how to jump on the wind's back, and then away we go — and if there are more winds than one they toss you about in the sky — they fling you miles and miles — but you always fall soft on to another wind — and sometimes you go crashing through the tops of trees, scaring the owls — and if you meet a boy's kite in the air you shove your foot through it. The stars are giving a party tonight! Oh, Wendy, when you are sleeping in your silly bed you might be flying about with me playing hide and seek with the stars! And Wendy, there are mermaids.
WENDY.   Mermaids, with tails?
PETER.   Such long tails.
WENDY.   Oh, to see a mermaid. *(She just succeeds in remaining on the nursery floor.)*
PETER.   Wendy, you could tuck us in at night.
WENDY.   Oo!
PETER.   None of us has ever been tucked in at night.
WENDY.   Oo!
PETER.   And make pockets for us. None of us has any pock-

ets. Wendy, how we should all respect you. *(At this she strikes her colours.)*

WENDY.   Of course, it's awfully fas-cin-a-ting! Would you teach John and Michael to fly too?

PETER.   *(Indifferently.)* If you like.

WENDY.   I don't promise to go away with you. I don't think there's the least chance of my going.

PETER.   *(Craftily.)* All right.

WENDY.   *(Playing rum-tum on John.)* John, wake up. There is a boy here who is to teach us to fly.

JOHN.   Is there? Then I shall get up. *(He raises his head from the floor.)* Hullo, I am up.

WENDY.   Michael, open your eyes. This boy is to teach us to fly. *(The sleepers are at once as awake as their father's razor; but before a question can be asked Nana's bark is heard.)*

JOHN.   *(To Peter.)* Quick, hide! Out with the light! *(They arrange their bedclothes to resemble their own sleeping bodies, and then hide in the bathroom or behind the curtains. When Liza enters with a firm hand on the troubled Nana's chain, the room is in comparative darkness.)*

LIZA.   There, you suspicious brute, they are perfectly safe, aren't they? Every one of the little angels sound asleep in bed. Listen to their gentle breathing. *(Nana's sense of smell here helps to her undoing instead of hindering it. She knows that they are in the room. Michael, who is behind the curtain window, is so encouraged by Liza's last remark that he breathes too loudly. Nana knows that kind of breathing, and tries to break from her keeper's control.)* No more of it, Nana. *(Wagging a finger at her.)* I warn you if you bark again I shall go straight for master and missus and bring them home from the party, and then won't the master whip you just! Come along, you naughty dog. *(The unhappy Nana is led away. The children emerge exulting from their various hiding-places. In their brief absence from the scene strange things have been done to them; but it is not for us to reveal a mysterious secret of the stage. They look just the same.)*

JOHN.   I say, can you really fly?

PETER.   Look! *(He is now over their heads.)*

JOHN.   How splendid!

WENDY.   Oh, how sweet!

PETER.   I'm sweet, oh, I am sweet! *(It looks so easy that they try it first from the floor and then from their beds, without encouraging results.)*

JOHN.   *(Rubbing his knees.)* How do you do it?

PETER.   *(Descending.)* You just think lovely wonderful thoughts and they lift you up in the air. Look. *(He is off again.)*

JOHN.   You are so nippy at it; couldn't you do it very slowly once? *(Peter does it slowly.)* I've got it now, Wendy. *(He tries; no, he has not got it, poor stay-at-home, though he knows the names of all the counties in England and Peter does not know one.)*

PETER.   I must blow the fairy dust on you first. *(Fortunately his garments are smeared with it and he blows some dust on each.)* Now, try; try from the bed. Just wriggle your shoulders this way, and then let go. *(The gallant Michael is the first to let go, and is borne across the room.)*

MICHAEL.   *(With a yell that should have disturbed Liza.)* I flewed! *(John lets go and meets Wendy near the bathroom door though they had both aimed in an opposite direction.)*

JOHN.   *(Tending to be upside down.)* How ripping!

WENDY.   Lovely!

MICHAEL.   *(Playing whack on a bed.)* I do like it!

THE THREE.   Look at me, look at me, look at me! *(They are not nearly so elegant in the air as Peter, but their heads have bumped the ceiling, and there is nothing more delicious than that.)*

JOHN.   *(Who can even go backwards.)* I say, why shouldn't we go out?

PETER.   There are pirates.

JOHN.   Pirates! *(He grabs his tall Sunday hat.)* Let us go at once! *(From down below in the street the lighted window must present an unwonted spectacle; the shadows of children revolving in the room like a merry-go-round. This is perhaps what Mr. and Mrs. Darling see as they come hurrying home from the party, brought by Nana who, you may be sure, has broken her chain. Peter's accomplice, the little star, has seen them coming, and again the window blows open.)*

PETER.   *(As if he had heard the little star whisper "cave.")* Now, altogether! *(Breaking the circle he flies out of the window, over the trees of the square and over the house-tops, and the others follow like a flight of birds.)* Second to the right, and straight on till morning! *(The broken-hearted mother arrives just in time to get a nip from Tink as she too sets out for the Never Land. Music. The nursery disappears from view and the four children are left flying through the night sky.)*

JOHN.   Come on, Michael, let's race. I'll give you a start.

MICHAEL.   Ow! Wendy!

WENDY.   What is it?

MICHAEL.   My head hurts.

PETER.   *(Diving past them.)* Well stop bumping into the clouds, silly!

JOHN.   *(To Wendy.)* I say, what a swank!

WENDY.   Do be more polite to him.

JOHN.   Then tell him to stop showing off. *(Half asleep. Michael begins to plummet earthwards.)* Michael!

WENDY.   Peter! Save him! *(Peter swoops down and returns with a dazed Michael.)* Oh, Peter, you're wonderful!

PETER.   Yes I am! What's your name?

WENDY.   I'm Wendy!

PETER.   I say, Wendy, if you see me forgetting you, just keep on saying "I'm Wendy" and then I'll remember. *(Peter soars away from them.)*

JOHN.   What a cheek!

WENDY.   You must be nice to him. What could we do if he were to leave us?

MICHAEL.   We could go back.

WENDY.   How could we ever find our way back without him?

JOHN.   Well then, we could go on.

WENDY.   That is the awful thing John. We should have to go on, for we don't know how to stop! *(The Storyteller appears in the darkness beneath them.)*

STORYTELLER.   So on, and on, and on they flew, over their second sea and through their third night, Peter teaching them how to sleep on the wind, and say fearfully funny things to the stars. And after many moons they drew near to the Never Land at last.

PETER.   There it is!

ALL.   What? Where? Where?

PETER.   The Never Land. Stand on tiptoe and you'll see it. *(They all stand on tiptoe in the air.)*

WENDY.   John! There's a lagoon!

JOHN.   Turtles, Wendy, burying their eggs in the sand!

MICHAEL.   I say, John, I see a flamingo with a broken leg!

JOHN.   Look, Michael, a cave!

WENDY.   John, what's that in the brushwood?

JOHN.   It's a wolf with her whelps!

MICHAEL.   I say, John, is that the smoke of a redskin camp?

JOHN.   Where? Show me! Are they on the warpath?

WENDY.   There, just across the mysterious river.

JOHN.   I see now. Yes, they're on the warpath right enough!

WENDY.   Michael, what's that?

MICHAEL.   It's a pirate ship! *(The air is suddenly rent by the most tremendous crash they have ever heard. The roar of it echoes through the mountains and the echoes seemed to cry savagely, "where are they, where are they, where are they?" Thus sharply do the terrified three learn the difference between an island of make-believe, and the same island come true. At last the heavens are steady again.)*

PETER.   Pirates!

JOHN.   *(To Michael.)* Are you shot?

MICHAEL.   I haven't tried yet.

PETER.   If you like we'll go down and kill one.

JOHN.   I say, do you kill many?

PETER.   Tons!

JOHN.   How ripping! Are there a lot of them?

PETER.   I've never known so many!

JOHN.   Who is captain now?

PETER.   Hook.

JOHN.   Jas. Hook?

PETER.   Aye.

JOHN.   *(Huskily.)* He was Blackbeard's bo'sun.

PETER.   Well, do you want an adventure now, or would you like to have your tea first?

ALL.   *(After a slight pause for thought.)* Tea first! *(They fly up and away.)*

END OF ACT ONE

ACT TWO

THE NEVER LAND

Enter the Storyteller. Behind him, the Never Land, shrouded in darkness. When the scene starts all is so dark that you scarcely know it has begun. This is because if you were to see the island bang (as Peter would say) the wonders of it might hurt your eyes. If you all came in spectacles perhaps you could see it bang, but to make a rule of that kind would be a pity. The first thing seen is merely some whitish dots trudging along the sward, and you can guess from their tinkling that they are probably fairies of the commoner sort going home afoot from some party and having a cheery tiff by the way. Then Peter's star wakes up, and in the blink of it, which is much stronger than in our stars, you can begin to make out the Never Land. You have often half seen it before, or even three-quarters, after the night-lights were lit, and you might then have beached your coracle on it if you had not always at the great moment fallen asleep.

STORYTELLER. What you see is the Never Land. You can make out masses of trees and you think you see wild beasts stealing past to drink, and mermaids basking in the lagoon beyond the trees, carefully combing their hair; not really far away for the Never Land is very compact, not large and sprawly with tedious distances between one adventure and another, but nicely crammed. It is summer time on the lagoon and winter on the river. *(This is not remarkable on Peter's island where all the four seasons may pass while you are filling a jug at the well.)* In the daytime you think the Never Land is only make-believe, and so it is to the likes of you, but this is the Never Land come true. *(Music. The island comes into full view, and the Storyteller walks about upon it.)* The beasts were out looking for the redskins, the redskins were looking for the pirates, the pirates were looking for the lost boys and they were all going round and round the island. Peter's home is at this very spot, but can you point out the way into it? Even if I told you which is the entrance? Even if I told you there were seven entrances? The holes in these seven tree-stumps are the "doors" down to Peter's home under the ground! He made seven because he thought seven boys must need seven doors! *(One of the lost boys emerges from his tree, perhaps driven from the abode below by companions less musical than himself.)* The biggest door belongs to the biggest boy, who is called Slightly and is quite possibly a genius. He cuts whistles out of the trees and then dances to his own tunes. *(Slightly plays his whistle, to which he capers entrancingly, with no audience save a Never ostrich which is also musically inclined. Unable to imitate Slightly's graces, the bird falls so low as to burlesque them and is driven from the entertainment. Tootles appears from his hole.)* Tootles is not the least brave, though the most unfortunate of the gallant band. He has been in fewer adventures than the others because the big things constantly happen while he has stepped around the corner. He will go off in some quiet hour to gather firewood and when he returns the others will be sweeping up the blood. *(Instead of souring his nature this has sweetened it and he is the humblest of the band.)*

TOOTLES.   Has Peter come back yet Slightly?

SLIGHTLY.   *(With a solemnity that he thinks suits the occasion.)* No, Tootles, no. *(Nibs appears.)*

STORYTELLER.   Nibs is more gay and debonair. *(And Curly.)* Curly is a pickle, and so often has he had to deliver up his person when Peter said "Stand forth the one who did this thing!," that he now stands forth whether he has done it or not. The other two are First Twin, *(First Twin emerges from his tree-stump.)* and Second Twin, *(And is joined by Second Twin from the next-door stump.)* who cannot be described because we should probably be describing the wrong one. There were six of them altogether, counting the twins as two, and tonight they were out awaiting their Captain's return. *(They are all dressed in the skins of animals they think they have shot, and so round and furry in them that if they fall they roll. Hunkering on the ground or peeping out of their holes, the six are not unlike village gossips gathered round the pump or like dogs waiting for the master to tell them that the day has begun.)*

CURLY. *(As if Peter might be listening.)* I do wish Peter would come back.

TOOTLES. I am always afraid of the pirates when Peter is not here to protect us.

SLIGHTLY. I am not afraid of pirates. Nothing frightens me. But I do wish Peter would come back and tell us whether he has heard anything more about Cinderella.

SECOND TWIN. *(With diffidence.)* Slightly, I dreamt last night that the Prince found Cinderella.

FIRST TWIN. *(Who is intellectually the superior of the two.)* Twin, I think you should not have dreamt that, for I didn't, and Peter may say we oughtn't to dream differently, being twins, you know.

TOOTLES. I am awfully anxious about Cinderella. You see, not knowing anything about my mother I am fond of thinking that she was rather like Cinderella. *(This is received with derision.)*

NIBS. All I remember about my mother is that she often said to father, "Oh, how I wish I had a cheque book of my own." I don't know what a cheque book is, but I should just love to give my mother one.

SLIGHTLY. *(Who is conceited, and thinks he remembers the days before he was lost with their manners and customs.)* My mother was fonder of me than your mothers were of you. *(Uproar.)* Oh yes, she was. Peter had to make up names for you, but my mother had wrote my name on the pinafore I was lost in. "Slightly Soiled"; that's my name. *(They fall upon him pugnaciously; not that they are really worried about their mothers, who are now as important to them as a piece of string, but because any excuse is good enough for a shindy. Not for long is he belaboured, for a sound is heard that is to send them scurrying for their holes.)*

PIRATES. *(From nearby.)*

Yo ho, yo ho, the pirate life,
The flag of skull and bones,

A merry hour, a hempen rope,
And hey for Davy Jones!

TOOTLES. Pirates! *(In a second of time the scene is bereft of human life. The only boy not to gain the safety of the underground home is Nibs, who is cut off from his tree-stump by the arrival of the first pirates.)*

STORYTELLER. What the lost boys have heard is a verse of the dreadful song with which the pirates stealthily trumpet their approach! A more villainous looking brotherhood of man never hung in a row on Execution Dock! *(The pirates come forward, one at a time, combing the landscape for any sign of the children.)* In advance of the rest with his ear to the ground is the handsome Italian Cecco, *(His great arms bare, pieces of eight in his ears as ornaments.)*

CECCO. ... who cut his name in letters of blood in the back of the governor of the prison at Gao.

STORYTELLER. Here is Bill Jukes, every inch of him tattooed.

JUKES. The same Jukes who got six lashes on the Walrus from Flint before he would drop the bag of gold moidores.

STORYTELLER. Cookson, said to be Black Murphy's brother —

COOKSON. But this was never proved!

STORYTELLER. And Gentleman Starkey, once an usher at a public school:

STARKEY. And still dainty in his ways of killing.

STORYTELLER. Skylights, *(Perched high in one of the trees as a look-out.)*

SKYLIGHTS. Morgan's Skylights!

STORYTELLER. — and the boatswain Smee, an oddly genial man, who stabbed, so to speak, without offense —

SMEE. — and the only non-conformist in Hook's whole crew!

STORYTELLER. Robert Mullins, famous for playing skittles with the mate of the Switch —

MULLINS. — for each others heads!

STORYTELLER. And Noodler, whose hands were, er ...

NODDLER. *(Smiling.)* ... fixed on backwards!

STORYTELLER.   But the cruelest jewel in this dark setting is Captain James Hook himself. *(Stately music, as Hook is borne forward on his great and sinister chair by four of his strongest men. He is gently lowered to the ground and sits in deepest solitude. Cadaverous and blackavised, he has an iron hook instead of a right hand, and it is with this he claws. The elegance of his diction and the distinction of his demeanor, show him one of a different class from his crew, a solitary among uncultured companions. A man of indomitable courage, the only thing at which he flinches is the sight of his own blood, which is thick and of an unusual colour. At his public school they said of him that he "bled yellow." In dress he apes the dandiacal associated with Charles II, having heard it said in an earlier period of his career that he bore a strange resemblance to the ill-fated Stuarts.)* His hair is dressed in long curls, like black candles about to melt. His eyes are blue as the forget-me-not, and of a profound melancholy, save when he claws, at which time two red spots appear in them. He's never more sinister than when he's most polite. Even his victims on the high seas note that he always says "sorry" when prodding them along the plank.

In his mouth a holder of his own contrivance enabling him to smoke two cigars at once. But those who have seen him in the flesh agree that the grimmest part of him, undoubtedly, is the iron claw. Such is the terrible man against whom Peter Pan is pitted. Which will win? *(Nibs is seen for a moment near the lagoon, and Starkey's pistol is at once upraised. The Captain twists his hook in him.)*

STARKEY.   *(Abject.)* Captain, let go!

HOOK.   Put back that pistol first!

STARKEY.   'Twas one of those boys you hate; I could have shot him dead.

HOOK.   Ay, and the sound would have brought Tiger Lily's redskins on us. Do you want to lose your scalp?

SMEE.   *(Wriggling his cutlass pleasantly.)* That is true. Shall I after him, Captain, and tickle him with Johnny Corkscrew? Johnny is a silent fellow.

HOOK.   Not now. He is only one, and I want to mischief all the seven. Scatter and look for them. *(The boatswain whistles his*

instructions and the men disperse on their frightful errand, continu-ing in their distasteful song.)
PIRATES.

Avast, belay, yo ho, heave to,

A-pirating we go.

And if we're parted by a shot

We're sure to meet below!

(With none to hear save Smee, Hook becomes confidential.)

HOOK.　　Most of all, I want their captain, Peter Pan. 'Twas he cut off my arm. I have waited long to shake his hand with this. *(Luxuriating.)* Oh, I'll tear him!

SMEE.　　*(Always ready for a chat.)* Yet I have oft heard you say your hook was worth a score of hands, for combing the hair and other homely uses.

HOOK.　　If I was a mother I would pray to have my children born with this instead of that. *(His left arm creeps nervously be-hind him. He has a galling remembrance.)* Smee, Pan flung my arm to a Crocodile that happened to be passing by.

SMEE.　　I have often noticed your strange dread of Croco-diles.

HOOK.　　*(Pettishly.)* Not of Crocodiles but of that one Croco-dile. *(He lays bare a lacerated heart.)* The brute liked my arm so much, Smee, that he has followed me ever since, from sea to sea, and from land to land, licking his lips for the rest of me.

SMEE.　　*(Looking for the bright side.)* In a way it is a sort of a compliment.

HOOK.　　*(With dignity.)* I want no such compliments; I want Peter Pan, who first gave the brute his taste for me. Smee, that Crocodile would have had me before now, but by a lucky chance he swallowed a clock, and it goes tick, tick, tick, tick inside him; and so before he can reach me I hear the tick and bolt. *(He emits a hollow rumble.)* Once I heard it strike six within him.

SMEE.　　*(Somberly.)* Some day the clock will run down, and then he'll get you.

HOOK.　　*(A broken man.)* Ay, that is the fear that haunts me. *(He rises.)* Smee, this seat is hot; odds, bobs, hammer and tongs, I am burning. *(He has been sitting, he thinks, on one of the island mushrooms, which are of enormous size. But this is a hand-painted one placed here in times of danger to conceal a chimney. They remove it, and tell-tale smoke issues; also, alas, the sound of children's voices.)*

SMEE.   A chimney!

HOOK.   *(Avidly.)* Listen! Smee, 'tis plain they live here, beneath the ground. There can be but one room below, for there is but one chimney. The silly moles had not the sense to see that they did not need a door apiece. This proves they have no mother! *(He replaces the mushroom. His brain works tortuously.)*

SMEE.   *(Hopefully.)* Unrip your plan, Captain.

HOOK.   To return to the boat and cook a large rich cake of jolly thickness with sugar on it, green sugar. We must leave the cake on the shore of the mermaids' lagoon. These boys are always swimming about there, trying to catch the mermaids. They will find the cake and gobble it up, because, having no mother, they don't know how dangerous 'tis to eat rich, damp cake. They will die!

SMEE.   *(Fascinated.)* It is the wickedest, prettiest policy ever I heard of.

HOOK.   *(Meaning well.)* Shake hands on't.

SMEE.   No, Captain, no. *(He has to link with the hook, but he does not join in the song.)*

HOOK.   Yo ho, yo ho, when I say "paw"
       By fear they're overtook,
       Naught's left upon your bones when you
       Have shaken hands with Hook!

(Frightened by a tug at his hand, Smee is joining in the chorus when another sound stills them both. It is a tick, tick as of a clock, whose significance Hook is, naturally, the first to recognize. "The Crocodile!" He cries, and totters from the scene. Smee follows. A huge Crocodile, of one thought compact, passes across, ticking, and oozes after them.)

STORYTELLER.   The wood is now so silent, you may be sure it is full of redskins — *(Enter Tiger Lily, her ear to the ground.)* This is Tiger Lily, the belle of the Piccaninny tribe, whose braves would all have her to wife but she wards them off with a hatchet. *(Tiger Lily beckons to the tribe to follow her.*

Enter Great Big Little Panther.) Next is Great Big Little Panther, a brave of so many scalps that in his present position they somewhat impede his progress. *(The rest of the tribe follow on and snake their way across the forest floor. Suddenly, they are as still as totems.)* Far away, across the lagoon, someone treads on a dry leaf!

TIGER LILY.   Pirates! *(They do not draw their knives. The knives slip into their hands.)* Have um scalps! What say Great Big Little Panther?

PANTHER.   Scalp um, oho, velly quick.

THE BRAVES.   *(In collaboration.)* Ugh, ugh, wah. *(A fire is lit and they dance round and over it till they seem part of the leaping flames. Tiger Lily invokes manitou; the pipe of peace is broken; and they crawl off like a long snake that has not fed for many moons. Emerging from his tree, Tootles peers after the tail and summons the other boys, who issue from their holes.)*

TOOTLES.   They are gone.

SLIGHTLY.   *(Almost losing confidence in himself.)* I do wish Peter was here.

FIRST TWIN.   H'sh! What is that? *(He is gazing at the lagoon and shrinks back.)* It is wolves, and they are chasing Nibs! *(The baying wolves are upon them quicker than any boy can scuttle down his tree.)*

NIBS.   *(Falling among his comrades.)* Save me, save me!

TOOTLES.   What should we do?

SECOND TWIN.   What would Peter do?

SLIGHTLY.   Peter would look at them through his legs; let us do what Peter would do. *(The boys advance backwards, looking between their legs at the snarling red-eyed enemy, who trot away foiled.)*

FIRST TWIN.   *(Swaggering.)* We have saved you, Nibs. Did you see the pirates?

NIBS.   *(Sitting up, and agreeably aware that the center of interest is now to pass to him.)* No, but I saw a wonderfuller thing, Twin. *(All mouths open for the information to be dropped into them.)* High over the lagoon I saw the loveliest great white bird. It is flying this way. *(They search the firmament.)*

TOOTLES.   What kind of a bird, do you think?

NIBS. *(Awed.)* I don't know; but it looked so weary, and as it flies it moans "Poor Wendy."

FIRST TWIN. *(Who has flown to a high branch.)* See, it comes, the Wendy! *(They all see it now.)* How white it is! *(A dot of light is pursuing the bird malignantly.)*

TOOTLES. That is Tinker Bell. Tink is trying to hurt the Wendy. *(He makes a cup of his hands and calls.)* Hullo, Tink! *(A response comes down in the fairy language.)* She says Peter wants us to shoot the Wendy.

NIBS. Let us do what Peter wishes.

SLIGHTLY. Ay, shoot it; quick, bows and arrows.

TOOTLES. *(First with his bow.)* Out of the way, Tink; I'll shoot it. *(His bolt goes home, and Wendy, who has been fluttering among the tree-tops in her white night-gown, falls straight to earth. No-one could be more proud than Tootles.)* I have shot the Wendy; Peter will be so pleased. *(From some tree on which Tink is roosting comes the Tinkle we can now translate "you silly ass." Tootles falters.)* Why do you say that? *(The others feel that he may have blundered, and draw away from Tootles.)*

SLIGHTLY. *(Examining the fallen one more minutely.)* This is no bird; I think it must be a lady.

NIBS. *(Who would have preferred it to be a bird.)* And Tootles has killed her.

CURLY. Now I see, Peter was bringing her to us. *(They wonder for what object.)*

SECOND TWIN. To take care of us? *(Undoubtedly for some diverting purpose.)*

ALL. *(Though every one of them had wanted to have a shot at her.)* Oh, Tootles!

TOOTLES. *(Gulping.)* I did it. When ladies used to come to me in dreams I said "Pretty mother," but when she really came I shot her! *(He perceives the necessity of a solitary life for him.)* Friends, goodbye.

SEVERAL. *(Not very enthusiastic.)* Don't go.

TOOTLES. I must; I am so afraid of Peter. *(He has gone a step or two toward oblivion when he is stopped by a crowing as of some victorious cock.)*

ALL. Peter! *(They make a paling of themselves in front of Wendy as Peter skims round the tree-tops and reaches earth.)*

PETER.   Greetings, boys! *(Their silence chafes him.)* I am back; why do you not cheer? Great news, boys, I have brought at last the thing we have all been waiting for, a mother for us all!

SLIGHTLY.   *(Vaguely.)* Ay, ay.

PETER.   She flew this way; have you not seen her?

SECOND TWIN.   Oh mournful day!

TOOTLES.   *(After making a break in the paling.)* Peter, I will show her to you.

THE OTHERS.   *(Closing the gap.)* No, no.

TOOTLES.   *(Majestically.)* Stand back, all, and let Peter see. *(The paling dissolves, and Peter sees Wendy prone on the ground.)*

PETER.   Wendy, with an arrow in her heart! *(He plucks it out.)* Wendy is dead. *(He is not so much pained as puzzled.)*

CURLY.   I thought it was only flowers that die.

PETER.   Perhaps she is frightened at being dead? *(None of them can say as to that.)* Whose arrow? *(Not one of them looks at Tootles.)*

TOOTLES.   Mine, Peter.

PETER.   *(Raising it as a dagger.)* O dastard hand!

TOOTLES.   *(Kneeling and bearing his breast.)* Strike, Peter; strike true.

PETER.   *(Undergoing a singular experience.)* I cannot strike; there is something stays my hand. *(In fact Wendy's arm has risen.)*

NIBS.   'Tis she, the Wendy lady. See, her arm. *(To help a friend.)* I think she said "Poor Tootles."

PETER.   *(Investigating.)* She lives! *(The delightful feeling that they have been cleverer than they thought comes over them and they applaud themselves. Holding up a button that is attached to her chain.)* See, the arrow struck against this. It is a kiss I gave her; it has saved her life.

SLIGHTLY.   I remember kisses; let me see it. *(He takes it in his hand.)* Ay, that is a kiss.

PETER.   Wendy, get better quickly and I'll take you to see the mermaids. She is awfully anxious to see a mermaid. *(Tinker Bell, who may have been off visiting her relations, returns to the wood and, under the impression that Wendy has been got rid of, is whistling as gaily as a canary. She is not wholly heartless, but is so small that she has only room for one feeling at a time.)*

CURLY.   Listen to Tink rejoicing because she thinks Wendy is dead! *(Regardless of spoiling another's pleasure.)* Tink, the Wendy lives. *(Tink gives expression to fury.)*

SECOND TWIN.   *(Tell-tale.)* It was she who said you wanted us to shoot the Wendy.

PETER.   She said that? Then listen, Tink, I am your friend no more. *(There is a note of acerbity in Tink's reply; it may mean "Who wants you?")* Begone from me for ever. *(Now it is a very wet tinkle.)*

CURLY.   She is crying.

TOOTLES.   She says she is your fairy.

PETER.   *(Who knows they are not worth worrying about.)* Oh well, not for ever, but for a whole week. *(Tink goes off sulking, no doubt with the intention of giving all her friends an entirely false impression of Wendy's appearance.)* Now what shall we do with Wendy?

CURLY.   Let us carry her down into the house.

SLIGHTLY.   Ay, that is what one does with ladies.

PETER.   No, you must not touch her; it wouldn't be sufficiently respectful.

SLIGHTLY.   That is what I was thinking.

TOOTLES.   But if she lies there she will die.

SLIGHTLY.   Ay, she will die. It is a pity, but there is no way out.

PETER.   Yes, there is. Let us build a house around her! *(Cheers again, meaning that no difficulty baffles Peter.)* Leave all to me. Bring the best of what we have. Gut our house. Be sharp. *(They race down their trees. While Peter is engrossed in measuring Wendy so that the house may fit her, John and Michael, who have probably landed on the island with a bump, wander forward, so draggled and tired that if you were to ask Michael whether he is awake or asleep he would probably answer "I haven't tried yet.")*

MICHAEL.   *(Bewildered.)* John, John, wake up. Where is Nana, John?

JOHN.   *(With the help of one eye but not always the same eye.)* It is true, we did fly! *(Thankfully.)* And here is Peter. Peter, is this the place? *(Peter, alas, has already forgotten them, as soon maybe he will forget Wendy. The first thing she should do now that she is here is to sew a handkerchief for him, and knot it as a jog to his memory.)*

PETER.　*(Curtly.)* Yes.

MICHAEL.　Where is Wendy? *(Peter points.)*

JOHN.　*(Who still wears his hat.)* She is asleep.

MICHAEL.　John, let us wake her and get her to make supper for us. *(The boys emerge, with odd articles of furniture.)* John, look at them!

PETER.　*(Still house-building.)* Curly, see that these boys help in the building of the house.

JOHN.　Build a house?

CURLY.　For the Wendy.

JOHN.　*(Feeling that there must be some mistake here.)* For Wendy? Why, she is only a girl.

CURLY.　That is why we are her servants.

JOHN.　*(Dazed.)* Are you Wendy's servants?

PETER.　Yes, and you also. Away with them. *(In another moment they are woodsmen hacking at trees, with Curly as overseer.)* Slightly, fetch a doctor. All look the other way. *(Slightly reels and goes.)*

MICHAEL.　What's he to do?

TOOTLES.　Gone for the doctor.

JOHN.　A real doctor?

NIBS.　H'sh. *(Slightly returns professionally in John's hat.)*

PETER.　Please, sir, are you a doctor?

SLIGHTLY.　*(Trembling in his desire to give satisfaction.)* Yes, my little man.

PETER.　Please, sir, a lady lies very ill.

SLIGHTLY.　*(Taking care not to fall over her.)* Tut, tut, where does she lie?

PETER.　In yonder glade. *(It is a variation of a game they play.)*

SLIGHTLY.　I will put a glass thing in her mouth. *(He inserts a pretend thermometer in Wendy's mouth and gives it a moment to record its verdict.)*

TOOTLES.　Oh dear, I hope she is not no more. *(Slightly*

shakes the thermometer and then consults it.)
PETER. *(Anxiously.)* How is she?
SLIGHTLY. Tut, tut, this has cured her.
PETER. *(Leaping joyously.)* I am glad.
SLIGHTLY. Give her beef tea out of a cup with a spout to it, tut, tut. I will call again in the morning. Good evening.
ALL. Good evening. *(Slightly goes.)*
JOHN. It was Slightly, wasn't it?
TOOTLES. *(Indicating Peter.)* H'sh.
JOHN. Oh, I'm not afraid of him.
PETER. What did you say, John?
JOHN. Nothing.
SLIGHTLY. *(Reappearing.)* Has the doctor been?
TOOTLES. Yes.
SLIGHTLY. I'm sorry I missed him. *(Peter surveys the odd bits of furniture the boys have brought up from below.)*
PETER. *(With an already fading recollection of the Darling nursery.)* These are not good enough for Wendy. how I wish I knew the kind of house she would prefer!
FIRST TWIN. Peter, she is moving in her sleep.
TOOTLES. *(Opening Wendy's mouth and gazing down into the depths.)* Lovely!
PETER. Perhaps she's going to sing in her sleep. Oh, Wendy if you could sing the kind of house you would like to have. *(It is as if she had heard him.)*
WENDY. *(Without opening her eyes.)*

    If I had a little house
    It would be as small as small
    Little branches from the trees
    Would be made into a wall
    With a window in each one
    Just enough to see the sun.

(The boys repeat this verse and begin to build the house around Wendy. While still visible she sings a second verse.)

    That would make my little house
    Quite the nicest ever seen
    With its windows painted bright

And its roof of mossy green
And, I should have said before
Roses growing round the door.

(The boys repeat this verse too. By the time they have finished, such is the urgency of Peter's silent orders that they have knocked down trees, laid a foundation and put up the walls and roof, so that she is now hidden from view.)

PETER.   Windows! *(Curly rushes them in.)* Roses! *(Tootles arrives breathless with a festoon for the door. Thus springs into existence the most delicious little house for beginners.)*

FIRST TWIN.   I think it is finished.

PETER.   There is no knocker on the door. *(Tootles hangs up the sole of his shoe.)* There is no chimney; we must have a chimney. *(They await his deliberations anxiously.)*

JOHN.   *(Unwisely critical.)* It certainly does need a chimney. *(He is again wearing his hat, which Peter seizes, knocks the top off it and places on the roof. In the friendliest way smoke begins to come out of the hat.)*

PETER.   *(With his hand on the knocker.)* All look your best; the first impression is awfully important. *(He knocks, and after a dreadful moment of suspense, in which they cannot help wondering if anyone is inside, the door opens and who should come out but Wendy! She has evidently been tidying up a little. She is quite surprised to find that she has nine children.)*

WENDY.   *(Genteely.)* Where am I?

SLIGHTLY.   Wendy lady, for you we built this house.

NIBS and TOOTLES.   Oh, say you are pleased.

WENDY.   *(Stroking the pretty thing.)* Lovely, darling house!

FIRST TWIN.   And we are your children.

WENDY.   *(Affecting surprise.)* Oh?

ALL.   *(Kneeling, with outstretched arms.)* Wendy lady, be our mother! *(Now that they know it is pretend they acclaim her greedily.)*

WENDY.   *(Not to make herself too cheap.)* Ought I? Of course it is frightfully fascinating; but you see I am only a little girl; I have no real experience.

TOOTLES.   That doesn't matter. What we sorely need is just a nice motherly person.

WENDY.   Oh dear, I feel that is just exactly what I am.

ALL.   It is, it is, we saw it at once.

WENDY.   Very well then, I will do my best. *(In their glee they go dancing obstreperously round the little house, and she sees she must be firm with them as well as kind.)* Come inside at once, you naughty children, I am sure your feet are damp. And before I put you to bed and tuck you in, I have just time to finish the story of Cinderella. *(They all troop into the enchanting house, whose not least remarkable feature is that it holds them. The last one to go in is Wendy, who pauses briefly before she enters. The Storyteller enters with Liza, the Darlings' servant.)*

STORYTELLER.   Before Wendy went to sleep that night, for some strange reason she remembered Liza — *(Liza moves across the island, examining the little house.)* — who, of course, has no right to be here at all. But she has so few pleasures and is so young that we should just let her have a peep at the little house, so cozy and safe with a bright light showing through the blind. *(Liza goes. Peter comes out, and marches up and down with drawn sword.)* Peter kept watch outside that night, for the pirates could be heard carousing far away on the lagoon and the wolves were on the prowl. *(Peter sits down, leaning against the door of the little house.)* After a time he fell asleep, and some unsteady fairies had to climb over him on their way home from an orgy. *(A horde of fairies crosses the stage giggling and singing, amongst them Tinker Bell.)* Any other child in their way they would have mischiefed, but they just tweaked Peter's nose and passed on. *(The fairies disappear and on our last sight of Peter it is so dark that we just guess he is the little figure who has fallen asleep by the door.)*

END OF ACT TWO

ACT THREE

THE MERMAIDS' LAGOON

STORYTELLER. From that night on, adventure became a daily occurrence. The best we can do is to show you one of them, as a specimen of an average hour on the island. The difficulty is — which adventure to choose. Should we take the brush with the redskins at Slightly Gulch? Or Tiger Lily and the Mermaids' Lagoon? Or Peter's defiance of the lions? Or the tale of the rich damp cake? Which shall we choose? *(The Storyteller solicits preferences from members of the audience!)* Perhaps the best way would be to toss for it. *(He tosses a coin.)* The lagoon has won! *(He deals with any demonstration of disappointment in the audience, as the lagoon appears.)* It is the end of a long playful day on the lagoon. The sun's rays have persuaded him to give them another five minutes, for one more race over the waters before he gathers them up and lets in the moon. *(There are many mermaids here, going plop-plop, and one might attempt to count the tails did they not flash and disappear so quickly. At times a lovely girl leaps in the air seeking to get rid of her excess of scales, which fall in a silver shower as she shakes them off. From the coral grottoes beneath the lagoon, where are the mermaids' bedchambers, comes fitful music. One of the most bewitching of these blue-eyed creatures is lying lazily on marooners' rock, combing her long tresses and noting effects in a transparent shell.)* Peter and his band are in the water behind Marooners' Rock. *(They have tracked this mermaid as if she were a trout, and at a signal ten pairs of arms come whack upon the mermaid to enclose her. Alas, this is only what was meant to happen, for she hears the signal [which is the crow of a cock] and slips through their arms into the water. It has been such a near thing that there are scales on some of their hands. They climb onto the rock crest-fallen.)*

WENDY. Doesn't it seem odd, swimming about in one's clothes?

PETER.   No, just like dogs.

WENDY.   *(Preserving her scales as carefully as if they were rare postage stamps.)* I did so want to catch a mermaid.

PETER.   *(Getting rid of his.)* It is awfully difficult to catch a mermaid. *(The mermaids at times find it just as difficult to catch him, though he sometimes joins them in their one game, which is lazily blowing their bubbles into the air and seeing who can catch them. The number of bubbles Peter has flown away with! When the weather grows cold mermaids migrate to the other side of the world, and he once went with a great shoal of them half the way.)* They are such cruel creatures, Wendy, that they try to pull boys and girls like you into the water and drown them.

WENDY.   *(Too guarded by this time to ask what he means precisely by "like you," though she is very desirous of knowing.)* How hateful! *(She is slightly different in appearance now, rather rounder, while John and Michael are not quite so round. The reason is that when new lost children arrive at his underground home Peter finds new trees for them to go down by, and instead of fitting the tree to them he makes them fit the tree. Sometimes it can be done by adding or removing garments, but if you are bumpy, or the tree is an odd shape, he has things done to you with a roller, and after that you fit. The other boys are now playing King of the Castle, throwing each other into the water, taking headers and so on; but these two continue to talk.)*

PETER.   Wendy, this is a fearfully important rock. It is called Marooners' Rock. Sailors are marooned, you know, when their captain leaves them on a rock and sails away.

WENDY.   Leaves them on this little rock to drown?

PETER.   *(Lightly.)* Oh, they don't live long. Their hands are tied, so that they can't swim. When the tide is full this rock is covered with water, and then the sailor drowns.

WENDY.   How awful! *(Wendy is uneasy as she surveys the rock, which is the only one in the lagoon and no larger than a table. Since she last looked around a threatening change has come over the scene. The sun has gone, but the moon has not come. What has come is a cold shiver across the waters which has sent all the wiser mermaids to their coral recesses. They know that evil is creeping over the lagoon. Of the boys Peter is of course the first to scent it, and he has leapt*

71

to his feet before the words strike the rock.)
    "And if we're parted by a shot
    We're sure to meet below."

(The games on the rock and around it end so abruptly that several divers are checked in the air. There they hang waiting for the word of command from Peter. When they get it they strike the water simultaneously, and the rock is at once as bare as if suddenly they had been blown off it. Thus the pirates find it deserted when their dinghy strikes the rock and is nearly stove in by the concussion.)

SMEE.   Luff, you spalpeen, luff! *(They are Smee and Starkey, with Tiger Lily, their captive, bound hand and foot.)* What we have got to do is hoist the redskin onto the rock and leave her there to drown. *(To one of her race this is an end darker than death by fire or torture, for it is written in the laws of the Piccaninnies that there is no path through water to the happy hunting ground.)*

STORYTELLER.   The face of Tiger Lily is impassive; she is the daughter of a chief ...

STARKEY.   *(Chagrined because she does not mewl.)* No mewling. This is your reward for prowling around the ship with a knife in your mouth.

STORYTELLER.   ... and as a chief's daughter she must die. It is enough.

TIGER LILY.   *(Stoically.)* Enough said.

SMEE.   *(Who would have preferred a farewell palaver.)* So that's it! On the rock with her, mate.

STARKEY.   *(Experiencing for perhaps the last time the stirrings of a man.)* Not so rough, Smee; roughish, but not so rough.

SMEE.   *(Dragging her onto the rock.)* It is the Captain's orders. *(A stave has in some time past been driven into the rock, probably to mark the burial place of hidden treasure, and to this they moor the dinghy.)*

WENDY.   *(In the water.)* Poor Tiger Lily!

STARKEY.   What was that? *(The children bob.)*

PETER.   *(Who can imitate the Captain's voice so perfectly that even the author has a dizzy feeling that at times he was really Hook.)* Ahoy there, you lubbers!

STARKEY.   It is the Captain; he must be swimming out to us.

SMEE.   *(Calling.)* We have put the redskin on the rock, Captain.

PETER.   Set her free.

SMEE.   But, Captain —

PETER.   Cut her bonds, or I'll plunge my hook in you.

SMEE.   This is queer!

STARKEY.   *(Unmanned.)* Let us follow the Captain's orders. *(They undo the thongs and Tiger Lily slides between their legs into the lagoon, forgetting in her haste to utter her war cry, but Peter utters it for her, so naturally that even the boys are deceived. It is at that moment that the voice of the true Hook is heard.)*

HOOK.   Boat ahoy!

SMEE.   *(Relieved.)* It is the Captain. *(Hook is swimming, and they help him to scale the rock. He is in gloomy mood.)*

STARKEY.   Captain, is all well?

SMEE.   He sighs.

STARKEY.   He sighs again.

SMEE.   *(Counting.)* And yet a third time he sighs. *(With foreboding.)* What's up, Captain?

HOOK.   *(Who perhaps has found the large rich damp cake untouched.)* The game is up. Those boys have found a mother!

STARKEY.   Oh evil day!

SMEE.   What is a mother?

WENDY.   *(Horrified.)* He doesn't know!

HOOK.   *(Sharply.)* What was that? *(Peter makes the splash of a mermaid's tail.)*

STARKEY.   One of them mermaids.

HOOK.   Dost not know, Smee? A mother is — *(He finds it more difficult to explain than he had expected, and looks about him for an illustration. He finds one in a great bird which drifts past in a nest as large as the roomiest basin.)* There is a lesson in mothers for you! The nest must have fallen into the water, but would the bird desert her eggs?

PETER.   No, I wouldn't. *(Peter, who is now more or less off his head, makes the sound of a bird answering in the negative. The nest is borne out of sight.)*

STARKEY.　Maybe she is hanging about here to protect Peter? *(Hook's face clouds still further and Peter just manages not to call out that he needs no protection.)*

SMEE.　*(Not usually a man of ideas.)* Captain, could we not capture these boys' mother and make her our mother?

HOOK.　Obesity and bunions, 'tis a princely scheme. We will seize the children, make them walk the plank, and Wendy shall be our mother!

WENDY.　Never! *(Another splash from Peter.)*

HOOK.　What say you, bullies?

SMEE.　There is my hand on't.

STARKEY.　And mine.

HOOK.　And there is my hook. *(All swear.)* But I had forgot; where is the redskin?

SMEE.　*(Shaken.)* That is all right, Captain; we let her go.

HOOK.　*(Terrible.)* Let her go?

SMEE.　'Twas your own orders, Captain.

STARKEY.　*(Whimpering.)* You called over the water to us to let her go.

HOOK.　Brimstone and gall, what cozening is here? *(Disturbed by their faithful faces.)* Lads, I gave no such order.

SMEE.　'Tis passing queer.

HOOK.　*(Addressing the immensities.)* Spirit that haunts this dark lagoon tonight, dost hear me?

PETER.　*(In the same voice.)* Odds, bobs, hammer and tongs, I hear you.

HOOK.　*(Gripping the stave for support.)* Who are you, stranger, speak.

PETER.　*(Who is only too ready to speak.)* I am Jas. Hook, Captain of the Jolly Roger.

HOOK.　*(Now white to the gills.)* No, no, you are not.

PETER.　Brimstone and gall, say that again and I'll cast anchor in you.

HOOK.　If you are Hook, come tell me, who am I?

PETER.　A codfish, only a codfish.

HOOK.　*(Aghast.)* A codfish?

SMEE.　*(Drawing back from him.)* Have we been captained all this time by a codfish?

STARKEY.   It's lowering to our pride.

HOOK.   *(Feeling that his ego is slipping from him.)* Don't desert me, bullies.

PETER.   *(Top-heavy.)* Paw, fish, paw! *(There is a touch of the feminine in Hook, as in all the greatest pirates, and it prompts him to try the guessing game.)*

HOOK.   Have you another name?

PETER.   *(Falling to the lure.)* Ay, ay.

HOOK.   *(Thirstily.)* Vegetable?

PETER.   No.

HOOK.   Mineral?

PETER.   No.

HOOK.   Animal?

PETER.   *(After a hurried consultation with Tootles.)* Yes.

HOOK.   Man?

PETER.   *(With scorn.)* No.

HOOK.   Boy?

PETER.   Yes.

HOOK.   Ordinary boy?

PETER.   No!

HOOK.   Wonderful boy?

PETER.   *(To Wendy's distress.)* Yes!

HOOK.   Are you in England?

PETER.   No.

HOOK.   Are you here?

PETER.   Yes.

HOOK.   *(Beaten, though he feels he has very nearly got it.)* Smee, you ask him some questions.

SMEE.   *(Rummaging his brains.)* I can't think of a thing.

PETER.   Can't guess, can't guess! *(Foundering in his cockiness.)* Do you give it up?

HOOK.   Yes.

PETER.   All of you?

SMEE, STARKEY and HOOK.   Yes!

PETER.   *(Crowing.)* Well, then, I am Peter Pan! *(Now they have him.)*

HOOK.   Pan! Into the water, Smee. Starkey, mind the boat. Take him dead or alive!

PETER.   (*Who still has all his baby teeth.*) Boys, lam into the pirates! (*For a moment the only two we can see are in the dinghy, where John throws himself on Starkey. Starkey wriggles into the lagoon and John leaps so quickly after him that he reaches it first. The impression left on Starkey is that he is being attacked by the Twins. The water becomes stained. Here and there a head shows in the water. In the growing gloom some strike at their friends, Slightly getting Tootles in the fourth rib while he himself is pinked by Curly. It looks as if the boys are getting the worst of it, which is perhaps just as well at this point, because Peter, who will be the determining factor in the end, has a perplexing way of changing sides if he is winning too easily. Starkey and Smee, out-numbered and badly shaken, swim for the shore.*

Hook's iron claw makes a circle of black water round him from which the boys flee like fishes, clambering aboard the abandoned dinghy and rowing to safety. There is only one prepared to enter that dreadful circle. His name is Pan. Hook has risen to the rock to breathe, and at the same moment Peter scales it on the opposite side. The rock is now wet and slippery as a ball, and they have to crawl rather than climb. Suddenly they are face to face. Peter gnashes his pretty teeth with joy. Quick as thought he snatches a knife from Hook's belt and is about to drive it home, when he sees he is higher up the rock than his foe.)

HOOK.   Bad form! (*Peter gives the pirate a hand to help him up. Hook takes the offered hand — and bites it. Not the pain of this but its unfairness is what dazes Peter. It makes him quite helpless. Every child is affected thus the first time he is treated unfairly. All he thinks he has a right to when he comes to you to be yours is fairness. After you have been unfair to him he will love you again, but will never afterwards be quite the same boy. No one ever gets over the first unfairness; no one except Peter. He often meets it, but he always forgets it. That was the real difference between him and all the rest. So when he meets it now it is like the first time, and he can only stare, horrified.*

Hook seizes the advantage and claws twice. Peter is untouched, but in his bewilderment he rolls off the rock. Hook is triumphant, but not for long, for the Crocodile, whose tick has been drowned in the strife, suddenly rears its jaws, and Hook, who has almost stepped into

76

them, is pursued by it to land.

All is quiet on the lagoon now, not a sound save little waves nibbling at the rock, which is smaller than when we last looked at it, and far away cries of "Peter — Wendy" from the boys in the dinghy, whose hearts would sink it if they knew of the peril of Wendy and her Captain.

These two small figures are now on the rock, but they have fainted. A mermaid who has dared to come back into the stillness stretches up her arms and is slowly pulling Wendy into the water to drown her. Wendy starts up just in time.)

WENDY.   Peter! *(He rouses himself and looks around him.)* Where are we, Peter?

PETER.   We are on the rock, but it is getting smaller. Soon the water will be over it. Listen! *(They can hear the wash of the relentless little waves.)*

WENDY.   We must go.

PETER.   Yes.

WENDY.   Shall we swim or fly?

PETER.   Wendy, do you think you could swim or fly to the island without me?

WENDY.   You know I couldn't, Peter; I am just a beginner.

PETER.   Hook wounded me twice. *(He believes it; he is so good at pretending that he feels the pain, his arms hang limp.)* I can neither swim nor fly.

WENDY.   Do you mean that we shall both be drowned?

PETER.   Look how the water is rising! *(They cover their faces with their hands. Something touches Wendy as lightly as a kiss. With little interest.)* It must be the tail of the kite we made for Michael; you remember it tore itself out of his hands and floated away. *(He looks up and sees the kite sailing overhead.)* The kite! Why shouldn't it carry you? *(He grabs the tail and pulls, and the kite responds.)*

WENDY.   Both of us!

PETER.   It can't lift two. Michael and Curly tried. *(She knows very well that if it can lift her it can lift him also, for she has been told by the boys as a deadly secret that one of the things about him is that he is no weight at all. But it is a forbidden subject.)*

WENDY.   I won't go without you. Let us draw lots which is to stay behind.

PETER.   And you a lady, never! *(The tail is in her hands, and the kite is tugging hard.)* Goodbye, Wendy!

WENDY.   Peter! *(The kite draws her out of sight across the lagoon.)*

STORYTELLER.   Peter was alone on the lagoon. The waters rose still further, lapping over the rock, and he knew that it would soon be submerged. Pale rays of light tiptoed across the waters, and from the coral grottoes could be heard a sound, at once the most musical and the most melancholy in the world, the mermaids calling to the moon to rise. *(Peter is afraid at last, and a tremor runs through him, like a shudder passing over the lagoon. But on the lagoon one shudder follows another till there are hundreds of them, and he feels just the one.)*

PETER.   *(With a drum beating in his breast as if he were a real boy at last.)* To die will be an awfully big adventure. *(The lagoon is now suffused with moonlight. The water is over Peter's feet. The nest is borne nearer, and the Never Bird, after cooing a message to him, leaves it and sings her way upwards. Peter, who knows the bird language, slips into the nest, first removing the two eggs and placing them in Starkey's hat, which has been left on the stave. The hat drifts away from the rock, but he uses the stave as a mast. The wind is driving him towards the open sea. He takes off his shirt, which he had forgotten to remove while bathing, and unfurls it as a sail. His vessel tacks, and he passes from sight, victorious.)*

END OF ACT THREE

INTERVAL

ACT FOUR

THE HOME UNDER THE GROUND

STORYTELLER. We have now reached the evening that was to be known among the children as the Night of Nights, because of its adventures and their upshot. What you can see is the Home under the Ground with the children in it, and the wood above ground with the redskins on it! Below, the children are preparing their evening meal. Above, the redskins are guarding the children from the pirates. The only way of communication between these two parties is by means of the hollow trees. Slightly, being addicted when hot to the drinking of water, has swelled in consequence, and secretly scooped his tree for easier descent. I shall therefore use his. *(The Storyteller descends to the home under the ground. The house has an earthen floor, which is handy for digging in if you want to go fishing; and owing to there being so many entrances there is not much wall space. The table at which the lost ones are sitting is a board on top of a live tree trunk, which has been cut flat but has such growing pains that the board rises as they eat, and they sometimes have to pause in their meals to cut a bit more off the trunk. Their seats are pumpkins or the large gay mushrooms of which we have seen an imitation one concealing the chimney. There is an enormous fireplace which is in almost any part of the room where you care to light it, and across this Wendy has scratched strings made of fiber, from which she hangs her washing. There are also various tom-fool things in the room of no use whatever. Michael's basket bed is nailed high upon the wall as if to protect him from the cat, but there is no indication at present of where the others sleep. At the back between two of the tree trunks is a grindstone, and near it is a lovely hole, the size of a band-box, with a gay curtain drawn across it so that you cannot see what is inside.)* This little niche is Tink's withdrawing room and bedchamber, and it's just as well that you can't see inside, for everything is so exquisite that you could scarcely resist making off with something. The couch is a genuine Queen Mab, the mirror is a Puss-in-Boots, of which there are now only three, unchipped, known to the fairy dealers, and the chest-of-drawers is an authentic Charming the Sixth. Tink is within at present as one can guess from the glow, for though she has a chandelier from Tiddlywink's for the look of the thing, of course she lights her residence herself. She is probably wasting valuable time just now, wondering whether to put on the smoky blue or the apple blossom. *(First Twin moves from the group of children around the cooking-pot preparing their evening meal, and sits on a high stool on the other side of the room, putting on a dunce's cap.)* The dunce's cap is an invention of Wendy's, but not wholly successful, because everybody wants to be dunce. *(The children carry imaginary bowls over to the table and sit down to their meal.)* Normally their suppers consist chiefly of bread-fruit, tappa-rolls, yams, mammee apples, and banana splash, washed down with calabashes of poe-poe. But it is a pretend meal this evening, with nothing whatsoever on the table. *(They often have these suppers and like them on occasion as well as the other kind. The pretend meals are not Wendy's idea; indeed she was rather startled to find, on arriving, that Peter knew of no other kind, and she is not absolutely certain even now that he does eat the other kind, though no one appears to do it more heartily. He insists that the pretend meals should be partaken of with gusto, and we see his band doing their best to obey orders.*

All the boys except Peter are here, and Wendy has the head of the table, smiling complacently at their captivating ways, but doing her best at the same time to see that they keep the rules about hands-off-the-table, no-speaking-at-once, and so on. She is wearing romantic woodland garments, sewn by herself, with red berries in her hair which go charmingly with her complexion, as she knows; indeed she searched for red berries the morning after she reached the island. The boys are in picturesque attire of her contrivance, and if these don't always fit well the fault is not hers but the wearers', for they constantly put on each others' things if they put on anything at all. Michael is in his cradle on the wall. The meal suddenly erupts into hilarity and clatter.)

WENDY. *(Her fingers to her ears, for their chatter and clatter are deafening.)* Si-lence! Is your mug empty, Slightly?

SLIGHTLY. *(Who would not say this if he had a mug.)* Not quite empty, thank you.

NIBS. Mummy, he has not even begun to drink his poe-poe.

SLIGHTLY. *(Seizing his chance, for this is tale-bearing.)* I complain of Nibs! *(John holds up his hand.)*

WENDY. Well, John?

JOHN. May I sit in Peter's chair as he is not here?

WENDY. In your father's chair? Certainly not.

JOHN. He is not really our father. He did not even know how to be a father till I showed him. *(This is insubordination.)*

SECOND TWIN. I complain of John! *(The gentle Tootles raises his hand.)*

TOOTLES. *(Who has the poorest opinion of himself.)* I don't suppose Michael would let me be baby?

MICHAEL. No, I won't.

TOOTLES. May I be dunce?

FIRST TWIN. *(From his perch.)* No. It's awfully difficult to be dunce.

TOOTLES. As I can't do anything important would any of you like to see me do a trick?

ALL. No.

TOOTLES. *(Subsiding.)* I hadn't really any hope.

NIBS. *(The tale-telling breaks out again.)* Slightly is coughing on the table.

CURLY. The twins began with tappa rolls.

SLIGHTLY. I complain of Nibs!

NIBS. I complain of Slightly!

WENDY. Oh dear, I am sure I sometimes think that spinsters are to be envied.

MICHAEL. Wendy, I am too big for a cradle.

WENDY. You are the littlest, and a cradle is such a nice homely thing to have about a house. You others can clear away now. *(She sits down on a pumpkin near the fire to her usual occupation, darning.)* Every heel with a hole in it! *(The boys clear away with dispatch, washing dishes they don't have in a non-existent sink and stowing them in a cupboard that isn't there. Instead of saw-*

81

ing the table-leg tonight they crush it into the ground like a concertina, and are now ready for play, in which they indulge hilariously.

A movement of the Indians draws our attention to the scene above. Hitherto, with the exception of Panther, who sits on guard on top of the little house, they have been hunkering in their blankets, mute but picturesque; now all rise and prostrate themselves before the majestic figure of Peter, who approaches through the forest carrying a gun and game bag. It is not exactly a gun. He often wanders away alone with this weapon, and when he comes back you are never absolutely certain whether he has had an adventure or not. He may have forgotten about it so completely that he says nothing about it; and then when you go out you find the body. On the other hand he may say a great deal about it, and tells Wendy, as a thing of no importance, that he got these marks from the little people for cheeking them at a fairy wedding, and she listens politely, but she is never quite sure, you know; indeed the only one who is sure about anything on the island is Peter.)

PETER.   The Great White Father is glad to see the Piccaninny braves protecting his wigwam from the pirates.

TIGER LILY.   The Great White Father save me from pirates. Me his velly nice friend now; no let pirates hurt him.

BRAVES.   Ugh, ugh, wah! *(Tiger Lily takes Peter aside.)*

TIGER LILY.   Now we rub noses.

PETER.   Oh, all right.

TIGER LILY.   Tiger Lily wants to be your Wendy. Peter Paleface come with me. Be Great Indian White Chief and this your squaw.

PETER.   Desert Wendy — never!

TIGER LILY.   Me scalp you if you no nice to me!

PETER.   I don't care, Wendy is my only mother.

TIGER LILY.   Tiger Lily has spoken.

PANTHER.   Loola, loola! Great Big Little Panther has spoken!

LONE WOLF.   Lone Wolf has spoken!

PETER.   The Great White Father has spoken! And now shut up! *(He descends his tree, not unheard by Wendy.)*

WENDY.   Children, I hear your father's step. He likes you to meet him at the door. *(Peter scatters pretend nuts among them and watches sharply to see that they crunch with relish.)*

ALL. Nuts!

WENDY. Peter, you just spoil them, you know!

JOHN. *(Who would be incredulous if he dared.)* Any sport, Peter?

PETER. Two tigers and a pirate.

JOHN. *(Boldly.)* Where are their heads?

PETER. *(Contracting his little brows.)* In the bag.

JOHN. But ... *(No, he doesn't say it. He backs away.)*

WENDY. *(Peeping into the bag.)* They are beauties! *(She has learned her lesson.)*

FIRST TWIN. Father, we want to dance.

PETER. Dance away, my little man.

SECOND TWIN. But we want you to dance.

PETER. Me, my old bones would rattle.

CURLY. And mummy too.

WENDY. The mother of such an armful dance!

SLIGHTLY. As it is Saturday night? *(They have long lost count of the days, but always if they want to do anything special they say this is Saturday night, and then they do it.)*

WENDY. Of course it is Saturday night, Peter?

PETER. People of our figure, Wendy?

WENDY. And it is only among our own progeny. *(He shrugs an indifferent assent.)*

PETER. True, true.

WENDY. On with your nighties first. *(They disappear into various recesses, and Peter and Wendy with her darning are left by the fire to dodder parentally.)* Dear Peter, with such a large family I have passed my best, but you don't want to change me, do you?

PETER. No. *(She is too loving not to know that he is not loving enough, and she hesitates as one who knows the answer to her question.)*

WENDY. What is wrong, Peter?

PETER. *(Scared.)* It is only pretend, isn't it, that I am their father?

WENDY. *(Drooping.)* Oh yes. *(His sigh of relief is without con-*

sideration for her feelings.) But they are ours, Peter, yours and mine.

PETER. *(Determined to get at facts, the only things that puzzle him.)* But not really?

WENDY. Not if you don't wish it.

PETER. I don't.

WENDY. *(Knowing she ought not to probe but driven to it by something within.)* What are your exact feelings for me, Peter?

PETER. *(In the classroom.)* Those of a devoted son, Wendy.

WENDY. *(Turning away.)* I thought so.

PETER. You are so puzzling. Tiger Lily is just the same; there is something or other she wants to be to me, but she says it is not my mother.

WENDY. *(With spirit.)* No, indeed it isn't.

PETER. Then what is it?

WENDY. It isn't for a lady to tell.

PETER. Perhaps Tink will tell me.

WENDY. *(With spirit.)* Oh yes, Tink will tell you. She has no scruples. She hugs you openly — Tink's an abandoned little creature. *(The curtain of the fairy chamber opens slightly and Tink who has been eavesdropping tinkles a laugh of scorn.)*

TINK. I know I am, and like a true woman, I glory in it.

PETER. She says she knows she's an abandoned little creature and that like a true woman, she glories in it. *(Badgered.)* I suppose that she wants to be my mother.

TINK. You silly ass!

WENDY. *(Who has picked up some of the fairy words.)* I almost agree with her! *(The boys all run in wearing their nightgowns and pajamas, and the dance begins. Such a deliciously creepy dance it is, in which they pretend to be frightened at their own shadows; little witting that so soon shadows will close in upon them, from whom they will shrink in real fear. So uproariously gay is the dance, as they buffet each other on the bed and out of it! First Twin is the best dancer and performs mightily on the bed and in it and out of it and over it to an accompaniment of pillow fights by the less agile; and then there is a rush at Wendy.)*

NIBS. Now the story you promised to tell us as soon as we were in bed!

WENDY.   (*Severely.*) As far as I can see you are not in bed yet. (*At last we see how they sleep, for in a babel the great bed which stands on end by day against the wall is unloosed from custody and lowered to the floor. Though large, it is a tight fit for so many boys, and Wendy has made a rule that there is to be no turning round until one gives the signal, when all turn at once. They scramble into the bed, and the effect is as a box full of sardines. Drawing up her stool.*) Well, there was once a gentleman —

CURLY.   I wish he had been a lady.

NIBS.   I wish he had been a white rat.

WENDY.   You mustn't interrupt! There was a lady also —

FIRST TWIN.   Excuse my interrupting you, Mummy, but you say there was a lady. You mean that there is a lady also, don't you? (*Anxiously.*) She's not dead, is she?

WENDY.   Oh no.

TOOTLES.   I'm awfully glad she's not dead. Are you glad, John?

JOHN.   Of course I am.

TOOTLES.   Are you glad, Slightly?

SLIGHTLY.   Rather!

TOOTLES.   Are you glad, Twins?

SECOND TWIN.   We are just glad.

WENDY.   The gentleman's name was Mr. Darling and the lady's name was Mrs. Darling —

JOHN.   I knew them!

MICHAEL.   (*Who was allowed to join the circle.*) I think I knew them.

WENDY.   They were married, you know; and what do you think they had?

NIBS.   White rats?

WENDY.   No, they had three descendants. White rats are descendants also. Almost everything is a descendant. Now these three children had a faithful nurse called Nana.

MICHAEL.   (*Alas.*) What a funny name!

WENDY.   But Mr. Darling — (*Faltering.*) Or was it Mrs. Darling — was angry with her and chained her up in the yard; so all the children flew away. They flew away to the Never Land, where the Lost Boys are.

CURLY. I just thought they did; I don't know how it is, but I just thought they did.

TOOTLES. Oh, Wendy, was one of the lost boys called Tootles?

WENDY. Yes, he was.

TOOTLES. *(Dazzled.)* Am I in a story? Wendy, tell us what Tootles did, tell us what Tootles said, tell us what Tootles was like! Nibs, I am in a story.

PETER. *(Who is by the fire making Pan's pipes with his knife and is determined that Wendy shall have fair play, however beastly a story he may think it.)* A little less noise there.

WENDY. *(Melting over the beauty of her present performance but without any real qualms.)* Now I want you to consider the feelings of the unhappy parents with all their children flown away. Think, oh think, of the empty beds. *(The heartless ones think of them with glee.)*

FIRST TWIN. *(Cheerfully.)* It's awfully sad.

WENDY. But our heroine knew that her mother would always leave the window open for her progeny to fly back by; so they stayed away for years and had a lovely time. *(Peter is interested at last.)*

FIRST TWIN. Did they ever go back?

WENDY. *(Comfortably.)* Let us now take a peep into the future. Years have rolled by, and who is this elegant lady of uncertain age alighting at London station? *(The tension is unbearable.)*

NIBS. Oh, Wendy, who is she?

WENDY. *(Swelling.)* Can it be – yes – no – yes, it is the fair Wendy!

TOOTLES. I am glad. Are you glad, Slightly?

WENDY. Who are the two noble portly figures accompanying her, now grown to man's estate? Can they be John and Michael? They are. *(Pride of Michael.)* "See, dear brothers," says Wendy, pointing upward, "there is the window standing open." So up they flew to their loving parents, and pen cannot inscribe the happy scene over which we draw a veil. *(Her triumph is spoilt by a groan from Peter and she hurries to him.)* Peter, what is it? *(Thinking he is ill and looking lower than his chest.)* Where is it?

PETER.   It isn't that kind of pain. Wendy, you are wrong about mothers. I thought like you about the window, so I flew back, but the window was barred, for my mother had forgotten all about me and there was another little boy sleeping in my bed. *(This is a general damper.)*

JOHN.   Wendy, let us go home!

WENDY.   Are you sure mothers are like that?

PETER.   Yes.

WENDY.   John, Michael! *(She clasps them to her.)*

FIRST TWIN.   *(Alarmed.)* You are not to leave us, Wendy?

WENDY.   I must.

NIBS.   Not tonight?

WENDY.   I'm frightened to stay another moment. Peter, will you make the necessary arrangements? *(She asks it in the steely tones women adopt when they are prepared secretly for opposition.)*

PETER.   *(Coolly.)* If you wish it. *(He ascends his tree to give the redskins their instructions. The Lost Boys gather around Wendy.)*

TOOTLES.   If there is anything we could do, Wendy, to make you more comfortable.

CURLY.   We would darn our own stockings, Wendy.

SLIGHTLY.   We would build you a bigger house.

WENDY.   I love my little house!

FIRST TWIN.   It will be worse than before she came!

SLIGHTLY.   We shan't let her go!

NIBS.   Let's keep her prisoner.

WENDY.   *(With one of those inspirations women have, in an emergency, to make use of some male who need otherwise have no hope.)* Tootles, I appeal to you.

TOOTLES.   *(Leaping to his death if necessary.)* I am just Tootles and nobody minds me much, but the first who does not behave to Wendy like an English gentleman, I will blood him severely. What are you, Slightly?

SLIGHTLY.   English gentleman.

TOOTLES.   What are you, Nibs?

NIBS.   English gentleman

TOOTLES.   What are you, Curly?

CURLY.   English gentleman.

TOOTLES.   What are you, Twins?

TWINS.   English gentlemen.

WENDY.   Dear, dear boys! *(Peter returns.)*

PETER.   *(With awful serenity.)* Wendy, I told the braves to guide you through the wood as flying tires you so.

WENDY.   Thank you, Peter.

PETER.   Then Tinker Bell will take you across the sea.

TINK.   And drop her into it!

NIBS.   *(Fingering the curtain which he is not allowed to open.)* Tink, you are to get up and take Wendy on a journey.

TINK.   Shan't!

NIBS.   *(Star-eyed.)* She says she won't!

PETER.   *(Taking a step towards that chamber.)* If you don't get up, Tink, and dress at once —

TINK.   All right, Peter.

PETER.   She is getting up!

WENDY.   *(Quivering now that the time to depart has come.)* Dear ones, if you will all come with me, I feel almost sure I can get my father and mother to adopt you. *(There is joy at this, not that they want parents, but novelty is their religion.)*

NIBS.   But won't they think us rather a handful?

WENDY.   *(A swift reckoner.)* Oh no, it will only mean having a few beds in the drawing-room; they can be hidden behind screens on first Thursdays. *(Everything depends on Peter.)*

ALL.   Peter, may we go?

PETER.   *(Carelessly through the pipes to which he is giving a finishing touch.)* All right. *(They scurry off to dress for the adventure.)*

WENDY.   *(Insinuatingly.)* I'm going to give you your medicine before you go. Get your things, Peter.

PETER.   *(Skipping about and playing fairy music on his pipes, the only music he knows.)* I am not going with you.

WENDY.   Yes, Peter.

PETER.   No.

WENDY.   To find your mother.

PETER.   *(His pipes more riotous than ever.)* I just want always to be a boy and to have fun. *(The lost ones run back gaily, each one carrying a stick with a bundle on the end of it.)*

WENDY.   Peter isn't coming! *(All the faces go blank.)*

JOHN. *(Even John.)* Peter not coming!

TOOTLES. *(Overthrown.)* Peter, why not? *(Curly cries. There is a general fear that they are perhaps making the mistake of their lives.)*

PETER. Now then, no fuss, no blubbering. *(With dreadful cynicism.)* I hope you like your mothers! Are you ready, Tink?

TINK. Aye, aye!

PETER. Then lead the way. *(Tink darts up any tree, but she is the only one, for a terrible sound can be heard from above ground.)*

PIRATES. *(Slowly advancing on the circle of redskins.)*

   Yo ho, yo ho, the pirate life,

   The flag of skull and bones,

   A merry hours, a hempen rope ...

(The Pirates have now completely surrounded the Indians, who have known the pirate whereabouts since, early in the night, one of Smee's fingers crackled. The brushwood has closed behind their scouts as silently as the sand on the mole; for hours they have imitated the lonely call of the coyote; no stratagem has been overlooked, but alas, they have trusted to the pale-face's honour to await an attack at dawn, when his courage is known to be at its lowest ebb.)

STORYTELLER. Captain Hook has basely broken the two laws of Indian warfare, which are that the redskins should attack first and that it should be at dawn. If the braves would rise quickly they might still have time to scalp, but this they are forbidden to do by the traditions of their race, for it is written that they must never express surprise in the presence of the pale-face. Thus perish the flower of the Piccaninnies.

PIRATES. ... And hey for Davy Jones! *(The air above is suddenly rent with shrieks and the clash of steel. Though they cannot see, the boys know that Hook and his crew are upon the Indians. Mouths open and remain open, all in mute appeal to Peter. He is the only boy on his feet now, a sword in his hand, the same he slew Barbecue with; and in his eye is the lust of battle.*

We can watch the carnage that is invisible to the children. Hook falls upon the Indians pell-mell, and one cannot withhold a reluctant admiration for the wit that conceived so subtle a scheme and the fell genius with which it is carried out. Many of the Indians are slain, though not unavenged, for with Lone Wolf fall Alf Mason and Canary Robb, while other pirates to bite the dust are Black Gilmour and

Alan Herb. Chay Turley, who laughed with the wrong side of his mouth [having no other], is tomahawked by Panther, who eventually cuts a way through the shambles with Tiger Lily and a remnant of the tribe. This onslaught passes and is gone like a fierce wind.

The victors wipe their cutlasses, and squint, ferret-eyed, at their leader. He remains, as ever, aloof in spirit and in substance. He signs to them to descend the trees, for he is convinced that Pan is down there, and though he has smoked the bees it is the honey he wants. There is something in Peter that at all times goads this extraordinary man to frenzy; it is the boy's cockiness, which disturbs Hook like an insect. If you have seen a lion in a cage futilely pursuing a sparrow you will know what is meant. The pirates try to do their Captain's bidding, but the apertures prove to be not wide enough for them; Hook cannot even ram them down with a pole. He steals to the mouth of a tree and listens.)

PETER. *(Prematurely.)* All is over!

WENDY. But who has won?

PETER. 'Hst! If the Indians have won they will beat the tom-tom; it is always their signal of victory. *(Hook licks his lips at this and signs to Smee, who is sitting on it, to hold up the tom-tom. He beats upon it with his claw, and listens for results.)*

TOOTLES. The tom-tom!

PETER. *(Sheathing his sword.)* An Indian victory! *(The cheers from below are music to the black hearts above.)* You are quite safe now, Wendy. Boys, goodbye. All turn your backs so as not to see your captain cry. *(He resumes his pipes. The boys slowly leave their captain, and disappear towards their holes.)*

WENDY. Don't forget to change your flannels.

PETER. Oh, all right.

WENDY. And don't forget your medicine. *(She puts something into a shell and leaves it for Peter. It is only water but she measures it out in drops.)*

PETER. I won't forget.

WENDY. Peter, what are you to me? You are my — what?

PETER. Your son, Wendy.

WENDY. Oh, goodbye! *(The travellers start upon their journey little witting that Hook has issued his silent orders: a man to the mouth of each tree. As the children squeeze up they are plucked from their trees and trussed. The only one treated differently is Wendy, whom Hook greets with a flamboyant bow and then escorts on his arm with dreadful politeness.)*

STORYTELLER. Unaware of the tragedy being enacted above, Peter was so full of wrath against grown-ups, who as usual were spoiling everything, that he started breathing quick short breaths at the rate of about 5 to a second. He did this because there is a saying in the Never Land that every time you breathe a grown-up dies; and Peter was killing them off vindictively as fast as possible. Then he decided not to take his medicine, so as to grieve Wendy, and lay down on the bed, outside the coverlet, to vex her still more.

Then he nearly cried; but it struck him how indignant she would be if he laughed instead; so he laughed a haughty laugh and fell asleep in the middle of it. Sometimes, though not often, he had dreams, and they were more painful than the dreams of other boys. For hours he could not be separated from these dreams, though he wailed piteously in them. At such times Wendy used to soothe him, and, when he grew calmer, put him back to bed before he quite woke up, so that he shouldn't know of the indignity to which she had subjected him. But on this occasion he had fallen at once into a dreamless sleep. *(Hook returns, and he and Peter are now, as it were, alone on the island. Hook armed to the teeth, is searching noiselessly for some tree down which the nastiness of him can descend. Don't be too much alarmed by this; it is precisely the situation Peter would have chosen; indeed if the whole thing were pretend.... One of his arms droops over the edge of the bed, a leg is arched, and the mouth is not so tightly closed that we cannot see the little pearls.*

Hook finds the tree. It is the larger one set apart for Slightly. Down this the pirate wriggles a passage. In the aperture below, his face emerges and goes green as he glares at the sleeping child. Does no feeling of compassion disturb his somber breast? The man is not wholly evil. He has a thesaurus in his cabin, and is no mean performer on the flute. What really warps his mind is a presentiment that he is about to fail. This is not unconnected with a beatific smile on the face of the sleeper, whom he cannot reach owing to being stuck at the foot of the tree. He, however, sees the medicine shell within easy reach, and to Wendy's draught he adds from a bottle five drops of poison distilled when he was weeping from the red in his eye. The expression on Peter's face merely implies that something heavenly is going on. Hook worms his way upwards, and winding his cloak around him, as if to conceal his person from the night of which he is the blackest part, he stalks moodily towards the lagoon.) It was gone ten o'clock by the Crocodile and Peter slept on. *(A dot of light flashes past him and darts down the nearest tree, looking for Peter, only for Peter, quite indifferent about the others when she finds him safe.)*

TINK.   Peter! Peter! Wake up, Peter!

PETER.   *(Stirring.)* Who is that?

TINK.   *(In one long ungrammatical sentence.)* Peter it's me it's me all the redskins got sworded most of them and Hooky and the pirates bagged the boys and Wendy too as well.

PETER.   The redskins were defeated? Wendy and the boys captured by the pirates! I'll rescue her, I'll rescue her! *(He leaps first at his dagger, and then at his grindstone, to sharpen it. Tink alights near the shell, and rings out a warning cry.)*

TINK.   What's this, Peter?

PETER.   Oh, that is just my medicine.

TINK.   It's been poisoned.

PETER.   Poisoned? Who could have poisoned it? I promised Wendy to take it, and I will as soon as I've sharpened my dagger. *(Tink, who sees its red colour and remembers the red in the pirate's eye, nobly swallows the draught as Peter's hand is reaching for it.)* Why, Tink, how dare you drink my medicine! *(She flutters strangely round the room, answering him now in a very thin tinkle.)* What is the matter with you!

TINK.   It was poisoned, Peter, and now I'm going to be dead!

PETER.   It was poisoned, and you drank it to save my life! Tink, dear Tink, are you dying? *(He has never called her "dear Tink" before, and for a moment she is gay; she alights on his shoulder and gives his chin a loving bite.)*

TINK. *(Whispering.)* You silly ass! *(She falls on her tiny bed. The boudoir, which is lit by her, flickers ominously.)*

PETER. Her light is growing faint. If it goes out that means she is dead.

TINK. *(Very faint.)* If only children believed in fairies ...

PETER. Tink, I can't tell what you're saying.

TINK. Listen, you idiot, I'm trying to tell you — I'd get well if children believed in fairies.

PETER. You'd get well if children believed in fairies?

TINK. Some hope.

PETER. There aren't any children here, Tink.

TINK. Oh well.

PETER. Perhaps there are children somewhere dreaming of the Never Land. *(He stretches out his arms, to all the boys and girls of whom he is not one.)* Wherever you are, do you believe?

TINK. *(Sitting up in bed, terribly faint now.)* What do you think?

PETER. Do you believe in fairies? Don't let Tink die. Say that you believe! If you believe, clap your hands. *(Many clap. Some don't. A few hiss. Then perhaps there is a rush of Nanas to the nurseries to see what on earth is happening. But Tink is saved. First her voice grows strong; then she pops out of bed; then she is flashing through the room more merry and impudent than ever. She doesn't think of thanking those who believed, but she would have liked to get at the ones who had hissed.)* Oh thank you, thank you, thank you! And now to rescue Wendy! *(Peter ascends his tree as if he were shot up it.)*

STORYTELLER. The moon was riding in a cloudy heaven when Peter rose from his tree, and set out upon his perilous quest.

PETER. Hook or me this time!

STORYTELLER. He was frightfully happy! *(It is not such a night as Peter would have chosen. He had hoped to fly, keeping not far from the ground so that nothing unwonted should escape his eyes; but in that fitful light to have flown low would have meant trailing his shadow through the trees, thus disturbing the birds and acquainting a watchful foe that he was astir. There was no other course but to press forward in redskin fashion, at which happily he is an adept.)* On his way round the island, Peter passed the Crocodile, and noticed that it had stopped ticking. At first he thought this strange, then he realized that the clock had run down ... *(Peter starts tick-tocking in imitation of the Crocodile and exits stealthily, as the "Jolly Roger" appears.)*

End of Act Four

ACT FIVE

Scene 1

THE PIRATE SHIP

STORYTELLER.   One green light squinting over Kidd's Creek marked where the brig The Jolly Roger lay, low in the water; a rakish-looking craft, foul to the hull, every beam in her detestable, like ground strewn with mangled feathers. She was the cannibal of the seas, and floated immune in the horror of her name. *(Most of the pirates are carousing at present in the bowels of the ship, but on the poop Mullins is visible, in the only greatcoat on the ship, raking with his glass the monstrous rocks within which the lagoon is cooped. Starkey is leaning over a bulwark, silently surveying the sullen waves. He is bare-headed and is perhaps thinking with bitterness of his hat, which he sometimes sees still drifting past him with the Never Bird sitting on it. The only sound to be heard is made by Smee at his sewing machine, which lends a touch of domesticity to the night. Hook appears from his cabin at the back and prowls the deck, the double cigar holder in his mouth. With Peter surely at last removed from his path we, who know how vain a tabernacle is man, would not be surprised to find him bellied out by the winds of his success, but it is not so; he is still uneasy, looking long and meaninglessly at familiar objects, such as the ship's bell or long tom, like one who may shortly be a stranger to them. It is as if Pan's terrible oath "Hook or me this time" had already boarded the ship. Canary Robb is asleep on deck, yet even in his dreams rolling mechanically out of the way when Hook draws near.)*

HOOK.   *(Communing with his ego.)* How still the night is; nothing sounds alive. Now is the hour when children in their homes are abed; their lips bright-browned with the good-night chocolate, and their tongues drowsily searching for belated crumbs, housed insecurely on their shining cheeks. Compare with them the children on this boat, about to tragically walk the plank. Split my infinitives, but 'tis my hour of triumph! *(Clinging to this prospect he dances a few jubilant steps, but they fall below his usual form.)* I should be feeling deevy, and yet a premonition of impending doom embraces me inexorably like a closing umbrella, and some disky spirit compels me now to make my dying speech, lest when dying there may be no time for it. All mortals envy me, yet better perhaps for Hook to have had less ambition. Ah, good form, that is all that really matters. Fame, o fame, thou glittering bauble, what if the very ... *(Smee, engrossed in his labours at the sewing-machine, tears a piece of calico with a rending sound which makes the solitary Hook think for a moment that the untoward has happened to his garments.)* I am the only man whom Barbecue feared, and Flint himself feared Barbecue. But — is it quite good form to be so feared by any man? Yea, more disquieting, is it not bad form even to think about good form? That is where the canker gnaws. *(Another rending of the calico, and another checking of the breeches.)* No little children love me. 'Tis said they find Smee lovable. But an hour agone I found him letting the youngest of them try on his spectacles. But soft, if Smee is lovable, what can it be that makes him so? *(A terrible answer suddenly presents itself.)* Good form? *(With a cry of rage he raises his iron hand over Smee's head; but he does not tear, arrested by a further sudden reflection.)* To claw a man because he has good form, what would that be? Bad form! Yes, bi – carbonate of soda, yes, even the ... *(A third rending of the calico disturbs him, and he has a private consultation with Starkey, who turns him round and evidently assures him that all is well. The peroration of his speech is nevertheless for ever lost, as eight bells strike and his crew pour forth in Bacchanalian orgy. From the poop he watches their dance till it frets him beyond bearing.)* Quiet, you scugs, or I'll cast anchor in you! *(He descends to a barrel on which there are playing cards, and his crew stand waiting, as ever, like whipped curs.)* Are all the prisoners chained, so that they can't fly away?

JUKES. Ay, ay Captain.

HOOK. Then hoist them up.

STARKEY. *(Raising the door of the hold.)* Tumble up, you un-gentlemanly lubbers. *(The terrified boys are prodded up and tossed about the deck. Hook seems to have forgotten them; he is sitting by the barrel with his cards.)*

HOOK. *(Suddenly.)* So! Now then, you bullies, six of you walk the plank tonight, but I have room for two cabin-boys. Which of you is it to be? *(He returns to his cards.)*

TOOTLES. *(Hoping to soothe him by putting the blame on the only person, vaguely remembered, who is always willing to act as a buffer.)* You see, sir, I don't think my mother would like me to be a pirate. Would your mother like you to be a pirate, Slightly?

SLIGHLTY. I don't think so, Tootles. Would your mother like you to be a pirate, Nibs?

NIBS. I don't think so, Slightly. Would your mother like you to be pirates, Twins?

TWINS. We don't think so, Nibs. Would your ...

HOOK. Stow this gab! *(To John.)* You boy, you look as if you had a little pluck in you. Didst never want to be a pirate, my hearty?

JOHN. *(Dazzled by being singled out.)* Well, when I was at school I rather wanted to be a pirate. I thought I'd call my-self Red-handed Jack.

MICHAEL. *(Stepping into prominence.)* What would you call me if I joined?

HOOK. Blackbeard Joe.

MICHAEL. John, what do you think?

JOHN. Stop! Should we still be respectful subjects of King Edward?

HOOK. You would have to swear "down with King Edward!"

JOHN. *(Grandly.)* Then I refuse!

MICHAEL. And I refuse!

HOOK. That seals your doom. Bring up their mother. *(Wendy is driven up from the hold and thrown to him. She sees at the first glance that the deck has not been scrubbed for years.)* So, my beauty, you are to see your children walk the plank.

WENDY. *(With noble calmness.)* Are they to die?

HOOK. They are. Silence all, for a mother's last words to

her children.

WENDY.   These are my last words. Dear boys, I feel that I have a message to you from your real mothers, and it is this, "we hope our sons will die like English gentlemen." *(The boys go on fire.)*

TOOTLES.   I am going to do what my mother hopes. What are you going to do, Slightly?

SLIGHTLY.   I am going to do what my mother hopes. What are you going to do, Nibs?

NIBS.   I am going to do what my mother hopes. What are you going to do, Twins?

FIRST TWIN.   What my mother hopes. John, what are ...

HOOK.   Tie her up! Get the plank ready.

STARKEY.   *(Privately to Wendy.)* I'll save you if you promise to be my mother.

WENDY.   I'd almost rather have no children at all. *(Wendy is roped to the mast; but no one regards her, for all eyes are fixed upon the plank now protruding from the poop over the ship's side. A great change, however, occurs in the time Hook takes to raise his claw and point to this deadly engine. No one is now looking at the plank: for the tick, tick of the Crocodile is heard. Yet it is not to bear on the Crocodile that all eyes slew round, it is that they may bear on Hook. Otherwise prisoners and captors are equally inert, like actors in some play who have found themselves "on" in a scene in which they are not personally concerned.*

Even the iron claw hangs inactive, as if aware that the Crocodile is not coming for it. Affection for their Captain, now cowering from view, is not what has given Hook his dominance over the crew, but as the menacing sound draws nearer they close their eyes respectfully.

There is no Crocodile. It is Peter who has been circling the pirate ship, ticking as he flies far more superbly than any clock. He drops into the water and climbs aboard, warning the captives with upraised finger (but still ticking) not for the moment to give audible expression to their natural admiration. Only one pirate sees him, Wibbles of the eye patch, who comes up from below. John claps a hand on Wibbles's mouth to stifle the groan; four boys hold him to prevent the thud; Peter delivers the blow and the carrion is thrown overboard. We hear a splash.)

SLIGHTLY.   *(Beginning to count.)* One! *(Starkey is the first pirate to open his eyes, but not before Peter has slipped into the cabin. The ship seems to him to be precisely as when he closed them. He cannot interpret the sparkle that has come into the faces of the captives, who are cleverly pretending to be as afraid as ever. He little knows that the door of the dark cabin has just closed on one more boy. Indeed it is for Hook alone he looks, and he is a little surprised to see him.)*

STARKEY.   *(Hoarsely.)* It is gone, Captain! There is not a sound. *(The tenement that is Hook heaves tumultuously and he is himself again.)*

HOOK.   *(Now convinced that some fair spirit watches over him.)*
　　　Then here is to Johnny Plank —
　　　(Sings.) Avast, belay, the English brig
　　　We took and quickly sank,
　　　And for a warning to the crew
　　　We made them walk the plank!

(As he sings he capers detestably along an imaginary plank and his copy-cats do likewise, joining in the chorus.)
　　　Yo ho, yo ho, the frisky plank,
　　　You walks along it so,
　　　Till it goes down and you goes down
　　　To tooral looral lo!

(The brave children try to stem this monstrous torrent by breaking into the national anthem.)

STARKEY.   *(Paling.)* I don't like it, messmates!

HOOK.   Stow that, Starkey! *(Sings.)*
　　　Yo ho, yo ho, the frisky plank ... *(He suddenly turns to
　　　　　the children.)*
　　　Do you boys want a touch of the cat before you
　　　　　walk the plank?

(He is now more pitiless than ever now that he believes he has a charmed life.)

Fetch the cat, Jukes; it is in the cabin.

JUKES.   Ay, ay, sir. *(It is one of his commonest remarks, and it is only recorded now because he never makes another. The stage direction "exit Jukes" has in this case a special significance. But only the children know that some one is awaiting this unfortunate in the cabin, and Hook tramples them down as he resumes his ditty.)*

HOOK.   *(Sings.)* Yo ho, yo ho, the scratching cat
Its tails are nine you know,
And when they're writ upon your back,
You're fit to —
(The last words will ever remain a matter for conjecture, for from the dark cabin comes a curdling screech which wails through the ship and dies away. It is followed by a sound, almost more eerie in the circumstances, that can only be likened to the crowing of a cock.)
What was that?

SLIGHTLY.   *(Solemnly.)* Two! *(Cecco swings into the cabin, and in a moment returns, livid.)*

HOOK.   *(With an effort.)* What is the matter with Bill Jukes, you dog?

CECCO.   The matter with him is he is dead — stabbed.

MULLINS.   Bill Jukes' dead!

CECCO.   The cabin is as black as a pit, but there is something terrible in there: the thing you heard a-crowing.

HOOK.   *(Slowly.)* Cecco, go back and fetch me out that doodle-doo.

CECCO.   *(Unstrung.)* No, Captain, no. *(He supplicates on his knees, but his master advances on him implacably.)*

HOOK.   *(In his most syrupy voice.)* Did you say you would go, Cecco? *(Cecco goes. All listen. There is one screech, one crow.)*

SLIGHTLY.   *(As if he were a bell tolling.)* Three!

HOOK.   'Sdeath and oddfish, who is to bring me out that doodle-doo? *(No one steps forward.)*

STARKEY.   *(Injudiciously.)* Wait till Cecco comes out. *(The black looks of some others encourage him.)*

HOOK.   I think I heard you volunteer, Starkey.

STARKEY.   *(Emphatically.)* No, by thunder!

HOOK.   *(In that syrupy voice which might be more engaging when accompanied by his flute.)* My hook thinks you did. I wonder if it would not be advisable, Starkey, to humor the hook?

STARKEY.   I'll swing before I go in there.

HOOK.   *(Gleaming.)* Is it mutiny? Starkey is ringleader. Shake hands, Starkey. *(Starkey recoils from the hook. It follows him till he leaps overboard.)*

SLIGHTLY. Four!

HOOK. Did any other gentleman say mutiny? *(They indicate that they did not even know the late Starkey.)* I will bring out that doodle-doo myself. *(He raises a blunderbuss but casts it from him with a menacing gesture which means that he has more faith in the claw. With a lighted lantern in his hand he enters the cabin. Not a sound is to be heard now on the ship, unless it be Slightly wetting his lips to say "five." Hook staggers out. Unsteadily.)* Something blew out the light.

MULLINS. *(With dark meaning.)* Some – thing?

NOODLER. What of Cecco?

HOOK. He is as dead as Jukes. *(They are superstitious like all sailors, and Mullins has planted a dire conception in their minds.)*

COOKSON. They do say as the surest sign a ship's accurst is when there is one aboard more than can be accounted for.

NOODLER. I've heard he allus boards the pirate craft at last. *(With a dreadful significance.)* Has he a tail, Captain?

MULLINS. They say that when he comes it is in the likeness of the wickedest man aboard.

COOKSON. *(Clinching it.)* Has he a hook, Captain? *(Knives and pistols come to hand, and there is a general cry —)*

PIRATES. The ship is doomed! *(— but it is not his dogs that can frighten Jas. Hook. Hearing something like a cheer from the boys he wheels round, and his face brings them to their knees.)*

HOOK. So you like it, do you? By Caius and Balbus, bullies, here is a notion: open the cabin door and drive them in. Let them fight the doodle-doo for their lives. If they kill him we are so much the better; if he kills them we are none the worse. *(This masterly stroke restores their confidence; and the boys, affecting fear, are driven into the cabin. Once out of sight they give vent to a bloodcurdling cacophony of screams. Desperadoes though the pirates are, some of them have been boys themselves, and all turn their backs to the cabin and listen, with arms outstretched to it as if to ward off the horrors that are being enacted there.*

Inside the cabin Peter relieves the boys of their manacles, and steals out softly as a snowflake onto the poop. The screams continue from the cabin as he releases Wendy; and now it would be easy for them all to fly away, but it is to be Hook or him this time. He signs to her to hide, and with awful grimness folding her cloak around him, the hood over his head, he takes her place by the mast. The screams subside into a deathly silence. Peter crows.)

MULLINS.   The doodle-doo has killed them all!

SEVERAL.   The ship's bewitched. *(They are snapping at Hook again.)*

HOOK.   I've thought it out, lads; there is a Jonah aboard.

COOKSON.   *(Advancing upon him.)* Ay, a man with a hook. *(If he were to withdraw one step their knives would be in him, but he does not flinch.)*

HOOK.   *(Temporizing.)* No, lads, no, it is the girl. Never was luck on a pirate ship wi' a woman aboard. We'll right the ship when she has gone.

MULLINS.   *(Lowering his cutlass.)* It's worth trying.

HOOK.   Throw the girl overboard.

MULLINS.   *(Jeering.)* There is none can save you now, missy.

WENDY.   *(From behind the mast.)* There is one!

MULLINS.   Who is that?

PETER.   *(Casting off the cloak.)* Peter Pan, the avenger!

HOOK.   *(Throwing out a suggestion.)* Cleave him to the brisket.

NOODLER.   The ship's accurst!

PETER.   Up, boys, and at them! *(Armed with such weapons as they can lay their hands on the boys leap from their concealment in the cabin, and the clash of arms resounds through the vessel. Man to man the pirates are the stronger, but they are unnerved by the suddenness of the onslaught and they scatter, thus enabling their opponents to hunt in couples and choose their quarry. Some are hurled into the lagoon; others are dragged from dark recesses. There is no boy whose weapon is not reeking save Slightly, who runs about with a lantern, counting, ever counting.)*

WENDY.   *(Meeting with Michael in a moment's lull.)* Oh, Michael, stay with me, protect me!

MICHAEL.   *(Reeling.)* Oh, Wendy, I've killed a pirate!

WENDY.   It's awful, awful.

MICHAEL.   No, it isn't, I like it, I like it. *(He casts himself into the fray once more. One by one the pirates are despatched, un-*

til only Hook is left. The boys encircle him. Again and again they close upon him and again and again he hews a clear space.)

HOOK.   Back, back, you mice. It's Hook; do you like him? *(He lifts up Michael with his claw and uses him as a buckler. A terrible voice breaks in.)*

PETER.   Put up your swords, boys. This man is mine. *(Hook shakes Michael off his claw as if he were a drop of water, and these two antagonists face each other for their final bout. They measure swords at arms' length, make a sweeping motion with them, and bringing the points to the deck rest their hands upon the hilts.)*

HOOK.   *(With curling lip.)* So, Pan, this is all your doing!

PETER.   Ay, Jas. Hook, it is all my doing.

HOOK.   Proud and insolent youth, prepare to meet thy doom!

PETER.   Dark and canister man ...

TOOTLES.   Sinister!

PETER.   ... sinister man. Have at thee! *(Hook or Peter this time! They fall to without another word. Peter is a rare swordsman, and parries with dazzling rapidity, sometimes before the other can make his stroke. Hook, if not quite so nimble in wrist play, has the advantage of a yard or two in reach, but though they close he cannot give the quietus with his claw, which seems to find nothing to tear at. He does not, especially in the most heated moments, quite see Peter, who to his eyes, now blurred or opened clearly for the first time, is less like a boy than a mote of dust dancing in the sun. By some impalpable stroke Hook's sword is whipped from his grasp, and when he stoops to raise it a little foot is on its blade. There is no deep gash on Hook, but he is suffering torment as from innumerable jags.)*

BOYS.   *(Exulting.)* Now, Peter, now! *(Peter raises the sword by its blade, and with an inclination of the head that is perhaps slightly overdone, presents the hilt to his enemy.)* Good form!

HOOK.   'Tis some fiend fighting me! Pan, who and what art thou? *(The children listen eagerly for the answer, none quite so eagerly as Wendy.)*

PETER.   *(At a venture.)* I'm youth, I'm joy, I'm a little bird that has broken out of the egg.

HOOK.   To't again! *(He now has a damp feeling that this boy is the weapon which is to strike him from the lists of man; but the grandeur of his mind still holds and, true to the traditions of his flag, he fights on like a human flail. Peter flutters round and through and over these gyrations as if the wind of them blew him out of the danger zone, and again and again he darts in and jags. Hook is stung to madness.)* I'll fire the powder magazine. *(He disappears, they know not where.)*

CHILDREN.   Peter, save us! *(Peter, alas, goes the wrong way and Hook returns, with a smoking bomb in his hand. He places it on the hold.)*

HOOK.   *(With gloomy satisfaction.)* In two minutes the ship will be blown to pieces. *(They cast themselves before him in entreaty.)*

CHILDREN.   Mercy! Mercy!

HOOK.   Back, you pewling spawn! I'll show you now the road to dusty death. A holocaust of children, there is something grand in the idea! *(Peter flies over to the hold, picks up the bomb and tosses it overboard. It explodes. Hook has not really had much hope, and he rushes at his other persecutors with his head down like some exasperated bull in the ring. But with bantering cries they easily elude him. Where is Peter? The incredible boy has apparently forgotten the recent doings, and is sitting on a barrel playing his pipes. This may surprise others but does not surprise Hook. Lifting a blunderbuss he fires forlornly at Peter, but hits the barrel, which is hurled across the deck. Peter remains sitting in the air still playing his pipes. At the sight of this the great heart of Hook breaks.)*

CHILDREN.

(Singing.) Yo ho, yo ho, the frisky plank
You walks along it so.
Till it goes down and you goes down
To Davy Jones below!

(Hook climbs the bulwarks as the children sing their mocking refrain, and prostrates himself into the water, where the Crocodile is waiting for him, open mouthed. Hook knows the purpose of this yawning cavity, but after what he has been through he enters it like one greeting a friend.)

HOOK.   *(In the mouth of the Crocodile.)* Peter Pan, no words of mine can express my utter contempt for you.

PETER.   Jas. Hook, thou not wholly unheroic figure, farewell.

HOOK.   *(Disappearing from view.)* Floreat Etona! *(We see the ship once more. Peter is sitting in Hook's great chair, glaring at the other children, one finger crooked in the shape of a hook.)*

STORYTELLER.   For the children the lateness of the hour was almost the biggest thing of all. Wendy got them to bed in the pirates' bunks pretty quickly you may be sure. All but Captain Pan who strutted up and down on deck until at last he fell asleep under the stars. *(Wendy goes to Peter and holds him.)* He had one of his dreams that night and cried in his sleep for a long time, and Wendy held him tight. *(The ship, and Peter and Wendy disappear from view.)*

By two bells that morning they were all stirring their stumps; for there was a big sea running; they all donned pirate clothes, cut off at the knee, shaved smartly, and tumbled up, chewing tobacco. Captain Pan calculated that if this weather lasted they should strike the Azores about the 21st of June, after which it would save time to fly. We must arrive in England before these rubbishy children, so there's no time to lose ... *(The Storyteller dons flying helmet and goggles and takes to the air.)* As we leave those magic shores we can still just hear the sound of the surf and far below us the mermaids singing in the dark lagoon. *(The Never Ostrich appears below him and stalks slowly across the stage.)* The beasts are still out looking for the redskins, but the redskins are departing now, in search of happier hunting-grounds. *(Tiger Lily and Great Big Little Panther appear with a remnant of the tribe.)* Slightly had counted seventeen pirates killed on that Night of Nights, but he wasn't quite correct in his figures, for two had reached the shore ... *(Enter Smee, who watches the redskins as they disappear from view, and Starkey, who is following them, laden with papooses.)*

SMEE.   You, Starkey.

STARKEY.   It's me, Smee.

SMEE.   I thought you were drowned.

STARKEY.   No, Smee, I was captured by the redskins. The squaws make me carry all their babies.

SMEE.   It's a come-down for a pirate.

STARKEY.   I shall become vulgar.

SMEE.   Never. Oh, surely, never.

STARKEY.   What a go is life.

SMEE.   But always interesting.

STARKEY.   What was the Captain's fate?

SMEE.   I know not. I saw the Crocodile following him. But I'm not sure whether it got him. *(Enter Crocodile. Starkey starts away in fear.)* Have no fear, Starkey. *(Smee offers it an arm and a leg.)* He only eats swells.

STARKEY.   Captain? Are you there?

SMEE.   I don't think he's inside.

BOTH.   Captain?! *(They sing.)*

    Avast, belay, inside d'you hear?

    My Captain Hook, yo ho!

    Oh, are you still a pirate bold?

    Or have you gone below?

(The Crocodile vomits the hook.)

SMEE.   It has got him. O Tempora! O Morris!

STARKEY.   Goodbye Smee, thou plebeian but honest heart, goodbye!

SMEE.   So long, Starkey, thou gentlemanly character, fare-well! *(They depart in opposite directions. Smee takes the hook with him, and examines it for a moment. The Crocodile plods away like one who has lived his great hour and can afford to take the rest of his life more leisurely.)*

STORYTELLER.   ... and from that day forth, Smee wandered about the world in his spectacles, making a precarious living by saying he was the only man that Jas. Hook had feared. *(Exit Smee.)*

We are now returning to that desolate home from which three of our characters had taken heartless flight so long ago. Would it not serve them jolly well right if they came back and found that their parents were spending the weekend in the country? It would be the moral lesson they have been in need of ever since we met them! *(He flies up and away.)*

End of Act Five, Scene 1

Scene 2

THE NURSERY

*The old nursery appears again with everything as it was at
the beginning of the play, except that the kennel has gone
and the window is standing open. So Peter was wrong about
mothers; indeed there is no subject on which he is so likely
to be wrong.*

*Mrs. Darling is asleep on a chair near the window, her eyes
tired with searching the heavens. Nana is stretched out list-
less on the floor. She is the cynical one, and though custom
has made her hang the children's night things on the fire-
guard for an airing, she surveys them not hopefully, but
with some self-contempt.*

MRS. DARLING.   *(Starting up as if we had whispered to her
that her brats are coming back.)* Wendy! John! Michael! *(Nana lifts
a sympathetic paw to the poor soul's lap.)* Oh, Nana, it is only a
dream! I dreamt my children had come back! You have put
their night things out again! Oh, Nana, it has touched my
heart to see you do that night after night, as if you expected
my children to come back, but they will never come back! *(In
trouble the difference of station can be completely ignored, and it is
not strange to see these two using the same handkerchief. Enter Liza,
who in the gentleness with which the house has been run of late is
perhaps a little more masterful than of yore.)*
LIZA.   *(Feeling herself degraded by the announcement.)* Nana's dinner is served. *(Nana, who quite understands what are Liza's feelings, departs for the dining room with our exasperating leisureliness,
instead of running, as we would all do if we followed our instincts.)*
MRS. DARLING.   Is the master's own dinner ready yet, Liza?
LIZA.   Yes, it's here. *(She places a rather handsome dog bowl on*

the floor, together with a napkin and a knife and fork. Bursting forth.) I want to give notice!

MRS. DARLING. *(Pained.)* Oh, Liza, is it the stairs?

LIZA. No, ma'am, it's the master. To think I have a master as have changed places with his dog!

MRS. DARLING. *(Gently.)* Out of remorse, Liza. *(Interested cheers from the street.)*

LIZA. That is the cab fetching him back. I don't think it's respectable to go to his office in a kennel, with the street-boys running alongside cheering. *(Even this does not arouse her mistress, which may have been the honourable intention. The kennel is conveyed to its old place by a cabby and friend, and Mr. Darling scrambles out of it in his office clothes.)*

MR. DARLING. Thank you, my men. *(Giving Liza his hat loftily.)* If you will be so good, Liza. *(The cheering is resumed.)* It is very gratifying.

LIZA. *(Contemptuous.)* Lot of little boys.

MR. DARLING. *(With the new sweetness of one who has sworn never to lose his temper again.)* There were several adults today. *(She goes off scornfully with the hat and the two men, but he has not a word of reproach for her. It ought to melt us when we see how humbly grateful he is for a kiss from his wife, so much more than he feels he deserves. One may think he is wrong to exchange into the kennel, but sorrow has taught him that he is the kind of man who whatever he does contritely he must do to excess; otherwise he soon abandons doing it.)*

MRS. DARLING. *(Who has known this for quite a long time.)* What sort of a day have you had, George? *(He is sitting on the floor by the kennel.)*

MR. DARLING. There were never less than a hundred running round the cab cheering, and when we passed the Stock Exchange the members came out and waved. *(He is exultant but uncertain of himself, and with a word she could dispirit him utterly.)*

MRS. DARLING. *(Bravely.)* I am so proud, George.

MR. DARLING. *(Commendation from the dearest quarter ever going to his head.)* I have been put on a picture postcard, dear.

MRS. DARLING. *(Nobly.)* Never!

MR. DARLING.   And I've had six invitations to dinner from leaders of society.

MRS. DARLING.   All asking you to come in your kennel?

MR. DARLING.   *(Thoughtlessly.)* Ah, Mary we should not be such celebrities if the children hadn't flown away.

MRS. DARLING.   *(Startled.)* George, you are sure you are not enjoying it?

MR. DARLING.   *(Anxiously.)* Enjoying it! See my punishment: living in a kennel.

MRS. DARLING.   Forgive me, dear one.

MR. DARLING.   It is I who need forgiveness, always I, never you. And now I feel drowsy. *(He retires into the kennel.)* Won't you play me to sleep on the nursery piano? And shut that window, Mary dearest; I feel a draught.

MRS. DARLING.   Oh, George, never ask me to do that. The window must always be left open for them, always, always. *(Mrs. Darling moves from bed to bed lighting the night lights and crooning a lullaby just as she did on that fateful night so long ago. She turns down the gas and, quietly crying, she leaves the nursery to play her husband to sleep on the drawing-room piano. The truants alight on the sill, and enter the darkened room. John to his credit having the tired Michael on his shoulders. They have nothing else to their credit; no compunction for what they have done, not the tiniest fear that any just person may be awaiting them with a stick. The youngest is in a daze, but the two others are shining virtuously like holy people who are about to give two other people a treat.)*

MICHAEL.   *(Looking about him.)* I think I have been here before.

JOHN.   It's your home, you stupid.

WENDY.   There is your old bed, Michael.

MICHAEL.   I had nearly forgotten.

JOHN.   I say, the kennel!

WENDY.   Perhaps Nana is in it.

JOHN.   *(Peering.)* There is a man asleep in it.

WENDY.   *(Remembering him by his bald patch.)* It's father!

JOHN.   So it is!

MICHAEL.   Let me see father. *(Disappointed.)* He is not as big as the pirate I killed.

JOHN. *(Perplexed.)* Wendy, surely father didn't use to sleep in the kennel?

WENDY. *(With misgivings.)* Perhaps we don't remember the old life as well as we thought we did.

JOHN. *(Chilled.)* It is very careless of mother not to be here when we come back. *(The piano is heard.)*

WENDY. H'sh! *(She goes to the door and peeps.)* That is her playing! *(They all have a peep.)*

MICHAEL. Who is that lady?

JOHN. H'sh! It's mother.

MICHAEL. Then are you not really our mother, Wendy?

WENDY. *(With conviction.)* Oh dear, it is quite time to be back!

JOHN. Let us creep in and put our hands over her eyes.

WENDY. *(More considerate.)* No, let us break it to her gently. *(She slips between the sheets of her bed; and the others, seeing the idea at once, get into their beds. Then when the music stops they cover their heads. There are now three distinct bumps in the beds. Mrs. Darling sees the bumps as soon as she comes in, but she does not believe she sees them.)*

MRS. DARLING. I see them in their beds so often in my dreams that I seem still to see them when I am awake. *(She sits down and turns away her face from the bumps, though of course they are still reflected in her mind.)* So often their silver voices call me, my little children whom I'll see no more. *(Silver voices is a good one, especially about John; but the heads pop up.)*

WENDY. *(Perhaps rather silvery.)* Mother!

MRS. DARLING. *(Without moving.)* That is Wendy.

JOHN. *(Quite gruff.)* Mother!

MRS. DARLING. Now it is John.

MICHAEL. *(No better than a squeak.)* Mother!

MRS. DARLING. Now Michael. And when they call I stretch out my arms to them, but they never come, they never come! *(She stretches out her arms for the three little selfish children they would never envelop again. Yes, they did, they went round Wendy and John and Michael, who had slipped out of bed and run to her.)* George! George! *(Mr. Darling wakes to share her bliss. Nana comes rushing in, and Liza, to greet the homecomers.)*

TOOTLES. *(Appearing at the window.)* Wendy, we can't hold on to the rain spout any longer.

MRS. DARLING. *(Startled.)* Why, who ... what ...

WENDY. It's all right, Mummy, they're just a few motherless boys we've brought back with us.

MRS. DARLING. But, my love ...

WENDY. Come in boys. *(All come in, hat in hand and carrying their bundles. They stand timidly in a respectful row.)* Oh, Mummy, say you'll have them!

MRS. DARLING. Of course I will!

MR. DARLING. *(To Wendy.)* I must say, Wendy, that you don't do things by halves.

TOOTLES. Do you think we should be too much of a handful, sir? Because if so we can go away.

WENDY. Father!

NIBS. We could sleep doubled up.

WENDY. I always cut their hair myself.

MRS. DARLING. George!

MR. DARLING. *(Bursting into tears.)* I'm as glad to have them as you are, but they should have asked my consent as well as yours, instead of treating me as a cipher in my own house. *(All the boys gather round Mr. Darling, only Slightly holding back.)*

TOOTLES. I don't think he's a cipher. Do you think he's a cipher, Curly?

CURLY. No, I don't. Do you think he's a cipher, Nibs?

NIBS. No, I don't. Do you think he's a cipher, Twins?

TWINS. No, we don't. Do you think he's a cipher, Slightly? *(Although absurdly gratified, Mr. Darling is strangely irritated by these repetitious remarks.)*

MR. DARLING. Stow that!... I'm sorry. I dare say we could find space for you all in the drawing room, if you can be fitted in.

TOOTLES. We'll fit in, sir.

MR. DARLING. Then follow the leader. Mind you, I'm not sure that we have a drawing-room, but we pretend we have, and it's all the same. Hoop-la!

ALL. Hoop-la! *(He dances out of the room and they all dance out after him, save Slightly who remains behind, somewhat troubled.)*

LIZA.   What is the matter, boy?

SLIGHTLY.   My mother doesn't seem to be here.

LIZA.   Is your name Slightly Soiled?

SLIGHTLY.   Yes'm.

LIZA.   Then I am your mother.

SLIGHTLY.   How do you know?

LIZA.   *(The good-natured creature.)* I feel it in my bones. *(They follow the others, leaving Mrs. Darling alone in the nursery with her three children.)*

STORYTELLER.   There could not have been a simpler, happier family than the Darling family that night —

MRS. DARLING.   My Darlings! *(Peter's face appears at the window.)*

STORYTELLER.   — but there was none to see them except a strange boy who was staring in at the window. He had ecstasies innumerable that other children can never know; but he was looking through the window at the one joy from which he must be for ever barred.

VOICES.   *(Offstage.)* John, Michael! *(John and Michael run to join their friends. Wendy suddenly sees Peter at the window.)*

WENDY.   Peter! *(She runs to the window and lets Peter in. He sits on the window ledge.)*

STORYTELLER.   Mrs. Darling was the loveliest age for a woman but too old to see Peter clearly.

MRS. DARLING.   Peter, where are you? Let me adopt you too.

PETER.   Would you send me to school?

MRS. DARLING.   *(Obligingly.)* Yes.

PETER.   And then to an office?

MRS. DARLING.   I suppose so.

PETER.   Soon I should be a man?

MRS. DARLING.   Very soon.

PETER.   *(Passionately.)* Hands off, lady! I don't want to go to school and learn solemn things. No one is going to catch me, lady, and make me a man. I want always to be a boy and to have fun. *(So perhaps he thinks, but it is only his greatest pretend.)*

WENDY.   You will be rather lonely in the evenings, Peter!

PETER. *(Rather hurtfully.)* I shall have Tink.

WENDY. Oh, Peter! Tink can't go a twentieth part of the way round! Mother, may I go?

MRS. DARLING. *(Gripping her for ever.)* Certainly not. I have got you home again, and I mean to keep you.

WENDY. But he does so need a mother.

MRS. DARLING. So do you, my love. But Peter, I shall let her go to you once a year for a week to do your spring cleaning. *(Wendy revels in this, but Peter, who has no notion what a spring cleaning is, waves a rather careless thanks.)* Say goodnight, Wendy.

WENDY. Goodnight, Peter.

PETER. Goodnight, Wendy. *(Mrs. Darling is a little startled to feel a light touch on her cheek as Peter passes her by on the way to the window.)*

WENDY. *(Calling through the window after him.)* Peter! You won't forget me, will you, before next spring cleaning time comes? *(The Storyteller emerges, to stand beside the nursery.)*

STORYTELLER. Of course Peter promised; and then he flew away. He took Mrs. Darling's kiss with him. That kiss, which had been for no one else, Peter took quite easily. *(Mrs. Darling smiles to herself.)* Funny. But she seemed satisfied. *(She leaves the nursery, which darkens as she goes.)* Of course all the boys went to school; it is sad to say that the power to fly gradually left them. Want of practice they called it, but what it really meant was that they no longer believed. Michael went on believing in him longer than the other boys, though they jeered at him; so he was with Wendy when Peter came for her at the end of the first year. She flew away with Peter in the frock she had woven from leaves and berries in the Never Land, and he was exactly as fascinating as ever. But the week was over, oh, so quickly. *(Wendy and Peter are huddled together on the floor of the nursery. Michael is sitting on the end of his bed.)*

WENDY. Remember not to bite your nails.

PETER. All right!

WENDY. When you come for me next year, Peter — you will come, won't you?

PETER. Yes. *(Gloating.)* To hear stories about me!

WENDY.   It is so queer that the stories you like best should be the ones about yourself.

PETER.   *(Touchy.)* Well then?

WENDY.   Peter, I want to tell you something.

PETER.   *(Enthralled.)* Is it a secret?

WENDY.   Oh, Peter! When Captain Hook carried us away ...

PETER.   Who's Captain Hook? Is it a story? Tell it me!

WENDY.   Do you mean to say you've forgotten Captain Hook? And how you killed him and saved all our lives?

PETER.   I forget them after I kill them.

WENDY.   *(Wondering about her rival.)* I didn't see Tink this time.

PETER.   Who?

WENDY.   Tinker Bell! Your fairy!

PETER.   *(Carelessly.)* There are such a lot of them. I expect she is no more.

WENDY.   *(Pained.)* Oh, Peter, you forget everything.

PETER.   Everything except mother Wendy. *(The nursery darkens once more and the Storyteller comes back into view.)*

STORYTELLER.   But next year he did forget. She waited in a new frock because the old one simply would not meet; but he never came. *(We see Wendy huddled at the end of her bed, her eiderdown wrapped tightly around her. Michael is gazing forlornly out of the open window.)*

MICHAEL.   Perhaps he's ill.

WENDY.   You know he is never ill. *(Michael closes the window, and turns to Wendy.)*

MICHAEL.   Perhaps there is no such person, Wendy. *(Michael starts to cry and goes to Wendy for comfort.)*

STORYTELLER.   And then Wendy would have cried if Michael had not been crying. *(The nursery darkens once more and disappears from our view.)* Peter came next spring cleaning; and the strange thing was that he never knew he had missed a year. But that was the last time the girl Wendy saw him. She tried not to have growing pains and she felt untrue to him when she won a prize for general knowledge. But the years came and went without bringing the careless boy and Wendy – grew – up. You need not be sorry for her. She was one of the kind that likes to grow up. All of the boys were grown up and done for by this time; so it is scarcely worth while saying anything about them. *(As they are named the grown up boys cross the stage in adult attire.)* You may see the Twins, and Nibs every day going to an office, each carrying a little bag and an umbrella. Curly is up at Oxford. Michael is an engine driver. Slightly married a lady of title and so he became a lord. You see that judge in a wig coming out of the iron door? That used to be Tootles. The bearded man who doesn't know any stories to tell his children was once John. *(The last of the boys disappears and the nursery begins to creep back into view.)* Years rolled on again, and Wendy had a daughter. She was called Jane, and when she was old enough to ask questions they were mostly about Peter Pan, and Wendy told her all she could remember in the very nursery from which the famous flight had taken place. *(We can now see the nursery clearly. The kennel has disappeared and there is an electric light in place of the old gas light fitting of previous years. Jane can be seen asleep in Wendy's old bed, very like Wendy used to look when she was Jane's age.)* And then one night came the tragedy. It was the spring of the year, and the story had been told for the night, and Jane was now asleep in her bed. *(Wendy comes into the nursery. She is a beautiful woman and is rather grandly dressed for dinner in a very fashionable gown of the 1920s. She goes over to Jane's bed to light her night light. She is startled by a strange little face at the window and a hand groping as if it wanted to come in.)*

WENDY.   Peter! *(The window blows open, as of old, and Peter drops to the floor. Wendy, helpless and guilty, squeezes herself as small as possible.)*

PETER.   Hallo, Wendy.

WENDY.   *(Faintly.)* Hallo, Peter.

PETER.   Hallo! Where is John?

WENDY.   John — doesn't sleep here now.

PETER.   Is Michael asleep?

WENDY.   *(Hesitating.)* Yes. *(Horrified at herself.)* That isn't Michael.

PETER.   Hallo, is it a new one?

WENDY.   Yes.

PETER. Boy or girl?

WENDY. Girl.

PETER. Do you like her?

WENDY. Yes! *(Something inside of Wendy is crying, "woman, woman, let go of me." Faltering.)* Peter — are you expecting me to fly away with you?

PETER. Of course, that is why I've come. *(A little sternly.)* Have you forgotten that this is spring-cleaning time? Come on. I'm Captain!

WENDY. I can't come. I've forgotten how to fly.

PETER. I'll soon teach you again.

WENDY. Oh, Peter, don't waste the fairy dust on me.

PETER. *(A fear at last assailing him.)* What is it?

WENDY. I will turn on the light and then you can see for yourself.

PETER. *(Frightened — husky.)* Wendy, don't turn on the light. *(Wendy switches on the light and faces him. A bewildered understanding comes to him. She puts out her arms but he shrinks back.)* What is it? What is it?

WENDY. I am old Peter. I am ever so much more than twenty. I grew up long ago.

PETER. You promised not to!

WENDY. I couldn't help it. I am a married woman, Peter.

PETER. No, you're not.

WENDY. Yes, and the little girl in the bed is my baby.

PETER. No she's not. *(After a pause — fiercely.)* What does she call you.

WENDY. Mother.

PETER. Mother?

WENDY. Oh Peter, Peter! *(She knows not what to do, and rushes from the room in agony. Peter takes a step towards the sleeping child, with a little dagger in his hand upraised, then is about to fly away, then flings himself on the floor and sobs. Jane wakes up.)*

JANE. Boy, why are you crying? *(Peter jumps up, and crossing to the foot of the bed, bows to her in the fairy way. Jane impressed, bows to him from the bed.)*

PETER. Hallo.

JANE.   Hallo.

PETER.   My name is Peter Pan.

JANE.   Yes, I know.

PETER.   I came for my mother to take her to the Never Land to do my spring cleaning.

JANE.   Yes, I know. I've been waiting for you.

PETER.   Will you be my mother?

JANE.   Oh yes. *(Jane descends from the bed and stands by Peter's side, with the look on her face that he likes to see on ladies when they gaze at him. Wendy has returned to the room and is looking at them rather forlornly.)*

PETER.   And you'll come with me?

JANE.   If Mummy says I may.

WENDY.   Oh!

JANE.   He does so need a mother.

WENDY.   Yes, I know.

JANE.   May I Mummy?

WENDY.   May I come too?

PETER.   You can't fly!

JANE.   It's just for one week.

WENDY.   Oh, Peter, how I wish I could take you up and squdge you! *(He draws back.)* Yes, I know.

STORYTELLER.   In a sort of way he knows what she means by "yes, I know," but in most sorts of ways he doesn't. It has something to do with the riddle of his existence. If he could get the hang of it his cry might become "To *live* would be an awfully big adventure!," but he can never get the hang of it. Of course in the end Wendy let them fly away together, to the Never Land. *(Peter and Jane fly out of the nursery window.)*

PETER.   Second to the right and then straight on till morning!

STORYTELLER.   Our last glimpse of her shows her at the window, watching them receding into the sky until they were as small as stars.

WENDY.   *(Her hands reaching out, calling with all her might.)* Peter! *(The nursery and the house begin to disappear.)*

STORYTELLER.   As you look at Wendy you may see her hair becoming white and her figure little again, for all this happened long ago. Jane became a common grown up with a daughter called Margaret; and every spring cleaning time, except when he forgot, Peter came for Margaret and took her to the Never Land, where she told him stories about himself, to which he listened eagerly.

When Margaret grew up she had a daughter who was Peter's mother in turn, and she will have a daughter too, and thus it will go on, so long as children are young, and innocent ... and heartless!

Will you dream now of the Never Land in years to come? *(We see Peter, flying high above us. He produces his pipes and starts to play.)* He plays on and on and on, till we wake up.

THE END

A NOTE ON DESIGN

We have omitted an accurate description of John Napier's brilliant design for our production because it was of such complexity and size that very few theatre companies could possibly afford to construct it, or indeed to give it house room. In any event, there are many different possible design solutions for the play and no such thing as an unsuitable theatre for it. Wherever there is a stage, and an auditorium along with it, there *Peter Pan* can be performed. All you will need is a nursery with a window for Peter to fly in and for all the children to fly out, and a magical Never Land, fully described by Barrie in his stage direction at the beginning of Act Two, and which must be realized however you'd most like it to be! Perhaps the only rule in designing *Peter Pan* is that the Director and Designer should follow Barrie's advice to his actors — they "must wear a child's outlook on life as their only important adornment."

One word of warning. However you achieve your nursery, and your Never Land, get your flying sorted out first! Don't design the show and then wonder how to do the flying. If you do, you will inevitably find yourselves flying into the scenery. You would, indeed, be well advised to consult a firm of experts — those ingenious professionals who alone fully understand the secrets of the fairy dust.

NOTE ON MUSIC

We have not included Stephen Oliver's wonderful score in this publication of our version as there will no doubt be theatre companies who, for reasons of economy or artistry, will wish to use their own musical ideas. Stephen's score is, of course, available for rent to anyone who wants to use it, and it can be ordered from G. Schirmer, Inc., Business Rental and Performance Department, P.O. Box 572, 445 Bellvale Road, Chester, New York 10918. Attn: Ella Windfield. Telephone: 845-469-2271. Facsimile: 845-469-7544.

PROPERTY LIST

ACT ONE

Pipe (STORYTELLER)
Match (STORYTELLER)
3 night lights
Children's night clothes
Towel
Black ink bottle (for inking worn sleeve) (MR. DARLING)
White tie (MR. DARLING)
Clothes brush
Wax tapers (to light night lights)
Jug and washing bowl
Teddy bear (MICHAEL)
Peter's shadow (MRS. DARLING)
First medicine bottle (NANA)
Medicine spoon (NANA)
Medicine glass (WENDY)
Second medicine bottle (WENDY)
Nana's bowl
Piece of chocolate (MRS. DARLING)
Top hat (JOHN)
Hot water bottle
Soap (PETER)
Thimble (WENDY)
Acorn button (PETER)
Chain (WENDY)
"Pieces of eight" earrings (CECCO)
Spyglass

ACT TWO

Whistle, home-made (SLIGHTLY)
Schoolmaster's cane (STARKEY)
Chair carried on oars (HOOK)
Raft with cushions
Hook
Double cigar holder (CAPTAIN HOOK)
Pistol (STARKEY)
Cutlass (SMEE)
Boatswain's whistle
Knives (INDIAN BRAVES)
Bows and arrows (made of sized branches) (LOST BOYS)
Rope
House building materials (LOST BOYS)
Furniture for Wendy's house (LOST BOYS)
Roses
Sword (PETER)
Spectacles (MICHAEL)

ACT THREE

Dinghy
Bird's nest (NEVER BIRD)
Kite
2 eggs
Hat (STARKEY)

ACT FOUR

Blankets (INDIAN TRIBE)
Dunce's cap
Darning material (WENDY)
Socks with holes

Gun and game bag
Knife (PETER)
Fairy pipes (PETER)
Sticks with bundles (LOST BOYS)
Knives and tomahawks (INDIAN TRIBE)
Pirate weapons
Tom tom drum
Peter's medicine (WENDY)
Shell
Grindstone
Poison bottle with red poison (HOOK)

ACT FIVE

Scene 1
Sewing machine
Length of calico
Barrel
Rope for tying Wendy (PIRATES)
Plank (PIRATES)
Manacles for shackling Lost Boys (PIRATES)
Weapons (in cabin)
Blunderbuss (CAPTAIN HOOK)
Lantern (lighted) (CAPTAIN HOOK)
Cutlass (MULLINS)
Smoking bomb
Broom stick
Spy glass

Scene 2
Flying helmet (STORYTELLER)
Flying goggles (STORYTELLER)
Hook's hook (CROCODILE)
Dog bowl (LIZA)
Napkin (LIZA)
Knife and fork (LIZA)

Hat (MR. DARLING)
Dagger (PETER)
Fairy pipes (PETER)

SOUND EFFECTS

Cuckoo clock striking six
Tick tock of clock
The wash of small waves
Ship's bells

... and any other sounds you think might help you in your
theatrical adventure.

NEW PLAYS

★ **MONTHS ON END by Craig Pospisil.** In comic scenes, one for each month of the year, we follow the intertwined worlds of a circle of friends and family whose lives are poised between happiness and heartbreak. "...a triumph...these twelve vignettes all form crucial pieces in the eternal puzzle known as human relationships, an area in which the playwright displays an assured knowledge that spans deep sorrow to unbounded happiness." –*Ann Arbor News.* "...rings with emotional truth, humor...[an] endearing contemplation on love...entertaining and satisfying." –*Oakland Press.* [5M, 5W] ISBN: 0-8222-1892-5

★ **GOOD THING by Jessica Goldberg.** Brings us into the households of John and Nancy Roy, forty-something high-school guidance counselors whose marriage has been increasingly on the rocks and Dean and Mary, recent graduates struggling to make their way in life. "...a blend of gritty social drama, poetic humor and unsubtle existential contemplation..." –*Variety.* [3M, 3W] ISBN: 0-8222-1869-0

★ **THE DEAD EYE BOY by Angus MacLachlan.** Having fallen in love at their Narcotics Anonymous meeting, Billy and Shirley-Diane are striving to overcome the past together. But their relationship is complicated by the presence of Sorin, Shirley-Diane's fourteen-year-old son, a damaged reminder of her dark past. "...a grim, insightful portrait of an unmoored family..." –*NY Times.* "MacLachlan's play isn't for the squeamish, but then, tragic stories delivered at such an unrelenting fever pitch rarely are." –*Variety.* [1M, 1W, 1 boy] ISBN: 0-8222-1844-5

★ **[SIC] by Melissa James Gibson.** In adjacent apartments three young, ambitious neighbors come together to discuss, flirt, argue, share their dreams and plan their futures with unequal degrees of deep hopefulness and abject despair. "A work...concerned with the sound and power of language..." –*NY Times.* "...a wonderfully original take on urban friendship and the comedy of manners—a *Design for Living* for our times..." –*NY Observer.* [3M, 2W] ISBN: 0-8222-1872-0

★ **LOOKING FOR NORMAL by Jane Anderson.** Roy and Irma's twenty-five-year marriage is thrown into turmoil when Roy confesses that he is actually a woman trapped in a man's body, forcing the couple to wrestle with the meaning of their marriage and the delicate dynamics of family. "Jane Anderson's bittersweet transgender domestic comedy-drama ...is thoughtful and touching and full of wit and wisdom. A real audience pleaser." –*Hollywood Reporter.* [5M, 4W] ISBN: 0-8222-1857-7

★ **ENDPAPERS by Thomas McCormack.** The regal Joshua Maynard, the old and ailing head of a mid-sized, family-owned book-publishing house in New York City, must name a successor. One faction in the house backs a smart, "pragmatic" manager, the other faction a smart, "sensitive" editor and both factions fear what the other's man could do to this house— and to them. "If Kaufman and Hart had undertaken a comedy about the publishing business, they might have written *Endpapers*...a breathlessly fast, funny, and thoughtful comedy ...keeps you amused, guessing, and often surprised...profound in its empathy for the paradoxes of human nature." –*NY Magazine.* [7M, 4W] ISBN: 0-8222-1908-5

★ **THE PAVILION by Craig Wright.** By turns poetic and comic, romantic and philosophical, this play asks old lovers to face the consequences of difficult choices made long ago. "The script's greatest strength lies in the genuineness of its feeling." –*Houston Chronicle.* "Wright's perceptive, gently witty writing makes this familiar situation fresh and thoroughly involving." –*Philadelphia Inquirer.* [2M, 1W (flexible casting)] ISBN: 0-8222-1898-4

DRAMATISTS PLAY SERVICE, INC.
440 Park Avenue South, New York, NY 10016 212-683-8960 Fax 212-213-1539
postmaster@dramatists.com www.dramatists.com

NEW PLAYS

★ **BE AGGRESSIVE by Annie Weisman.** Vista Del Sol is paradise, sandy beaches, avocado-lined streets. But for seventeen-year-old cheerleader Laura, everything changes when her mother is killed in a car crash, and she embarks on a journey to the Spirit Institute of the South where she can learn "cheer" with Bible belt intensity. "…filled with lingual gymnastics…stylized rapid-fire dialogue…" *–Variety*. "…a new, exciting, and unique voice in the American theatre…" *–BackStage West*. [1M, 4W, extras] ISBN: 0-8222-1894-1

★ **FOUR by Christopher Shinn.** Four people struggle desperately to connect in this quiet, sophisticated, moving drama. "…smart, broken-hearted…Mr. Shinn has a precocious and forgiving sense of how power shifts in the game of sexual pursuit…He promises to be a playwright to reckon with…" *–NY Times*. "A voice emerges from an American place. It's got humor, sadness and a fresh and touching rhythm that tell of the loneliness and secrets of life…[a] poetic, haunting play." *–NY Post*. [3M, 1W] ISBN: 0-8222-1850-X

★ **WONDER OF THE WORLD by David Lindsay-Abaire.** A madcap picaresque involving Niagara Falls, a lonely tour-boat captain, a pair of bickering private detectives and a husband's dirty little secret. "Exceedingly whimsical and playfully wicked. Winning and genial. A top-drawer production." *–NY Times*. "Full frontal lunacy is on display. A most assuredly fresh and hilarious tragicomedy of marital discord run amok…absolutely hysterical…" *–Variety*. [3M, 4W (doubling)] ISBN: 0-8222-1863-1

★ **QED by Peter Parnell.** Nobel Prize-winning physicist and all-around genius Richard Feynman holds forth with captivating wit and wisdom in this fascinating biographical play that originally starred Alan Alda. "QED is a seductive mix of science, human affections, moral courage, and comic eccentricity. It reflects on, among other things, death, the absence of God, travel to an unexplored country, the pleasures of drumming, and the need to know and understand." *–NY Magazine*. "Its rhythms correspond to the way that people—even geniuses—approach and avoid highly emotional issues, and it portrays Feynman with affection and awe." *–The New Yorker*. [1M, 1W] ISBN: 0-8222-1924-7

★ **UNWRAP YOUR CANDY by Doug Wright.** Alternately chilling and hilarious, this deliciously macabre collection of four bedtime tales for adults is guaranteed to keep you awake for nights on end. "Engaging and intellectually satisfying…a treat to watch." *–NY Times*. "Fiendishly clever. Mordantly funny and chilling. Doug Wright teases, freezes and zaps us." *–Village Voice*. "Four bite-size plays that bite back." *–Variety*. [flexible casting] ISBN: 0-8222-1871-2

★ **FURTHER THAN THE FURTHEST THING by Zinnie Harris.** On a remote island in the middle of the Atlantic secrets are buried. When the outside world comes calling, the islanders find their world blown apart from the inside as well as beyond. "Harris winningly produces an intimate and poetic, as well as political, family saga." *–Independent (London)*. "Harris' enthralling adventure of a play marks a departure from stale, well-furrowed theatrical terrain." *–Evening Standard (London)*. [3M, 2W] ISBN: 0-8222-1874-7

★ **THE DESIGNATED MOURNER by Wallace Shawn.** The story of three people living in a country where what sort of books people like to read and how they choose to amuse themselves becomes both firmly personal and unexpectedly entangled with questions of survival. "This is a playwright who does not just tell you what it is like to be arrested at night by goons or to fall morally apart and become an aimless yet weirdly contented ghost yourself. He has the originality to make you feel it." *–Times (London)*. "A fascinating play with beautiful passages of writing…" *–Variety*. [2M, 1W] ISBN: 0-8222-1848-8

DRAMATISTS PLAY SERVICE, INC.
440 Park Avenue South, New York, NY 10016 212-683-8960 Fax 212-213-1539
postmaster@dramatists.com www.dramatists.com

NEW PLAYS

★ **SHEL'S SHORTS by Shel Silverstein.** Lauded poet, songwriter and author of children's books, the incomparable Shel Silverstein's short plays are deeply infused with the same wicked sense of humor that made him famous. "...[a] childlike honesty and twisted sense of humor." –*Boston Herald.* "...terse dialogue and an absurdity laced with a tang of dread give [*Shel's Shorts*] more than a trace of Samuel Beckett's comic existentialism." –*Boston Phoenix.* [flexible casting] ISBN: 0-8222-1897-6

★ **AN ADULT EVENING OF SHEL SILVERSTEIN by Shel Silverstein.** Welcome to the darkly comic world of Shel Silverstein, a world where nothing is as it seems and where the most innocent conversation can turn menacing in an instant. These ten imaginative plays vary widely in content, but the style is unmistakable. "...[*An Adult Evening*] shows off Silverstein's virtuosic gift for wordplay...[and] sends the audience out...with a clear appreciation of human nature as perverse and laughable." –*NY Times.* [flexible casting] ISBN: 0-8222-1873-9

★ **WHERE'S MY MONEY? by John Patrick Shanley.** A caustic and sardonic vivisection of the institution of marriage, laced with the author's inimitable razor-sharp wit. "...Shanley's gift for acid-laced one-liners and emotionally tumescent exchanges is certainly potent..." –*Variety.* "...lively, smart, occasionally scary and rich in reverse wisdom." –*NY Times.* [3M, 3W] ISBN: 0-8222-1865-8

★ **A FEW STOUT INDIVIDUALS by John Guare.** A wonderfully screwy comedy-drama that figures Ulysses S. Grant in the throes of writing his memoirs, surrounded by a cast of fantastical characters, including the Emperor and Empress of Japan, the opera star Adelina Patti and Mark Twain. "Guare's smarts, passion and creativity skyrocket to awesome heights..." –*Star Ledger.* "...precisely the kind of good new play that you might call an everyday miracle...every minute of it is fresh and newly alive..." –*Village Voice.* [10M, 3W] ISBN: 0-8222-1907-7

★ **BREATH, BOOM by Kia Corthron.** A look at fourteen years in the life of Prix, a Bronx native, from her ruthless girl-gang leadership at sixteen through her coming to maturity at thirty. "...vivid world, believable and eye-opening, a place worthy of a dramatic visit, where no one would want to live but many have to." –*NY Times.* "...rich with humor, terse vernacular strength and gritty detail..." –*Variety.* [1M, 9W] ISBN: 0-8222-1849-6

★ **THE LATE HENRY MOSS by Sam Shepard.** Two antagonistic brothers, Ray and Earl, are brought together after their father, Henry Moss, is found dead in his seedy New Mexico home in this classic Shepard tale. "...His singular gift has been for building mysteries out of the ordinary ingredients of American family life..." –*NY Times.* "...rich moments ...Shepard finds gold." –*LA Times.* [7M, 1W] ISBN: 0-8222-1858-5

★ **THE CARPETBAGGER'S CHILDREN by Horton Foote.** One family's history spanning from the Civil War to WWII is recounted by three sisters in evocative, intertwining monologues. "...bittersweet music—[a] rhapsody of ambivalence...in its modest, garrulous way...theatrically daring." –*The New Yorker.* [3W] ISBN: 0-8222-1843-7

★ **THE NINA VARIATIONS by Steven Dietz.** In this funny, fierce and heartbreaking homage to *The Seagull*, Dietz puts Chekhov's star-crossed lovers in a room and doesn't let them out. "A perfect little jewel of a play..." –*Shepherdstown Chronicle.* "...a delightful revelation of a writer at play; and also an odd, haunting, moving theater piece of lingering beauty." –*Eastside Journal (Seattle).* [1M, 1W (flexible casting)] ISBN: 0-8222-1891-7

DRAMATISTS PLAY SERVICE, INC.
440 Park Avenue South, New York, NY 10016 212-683-8960 Fax 212-213-1539
postmaster@dramatists.com www.dramatists.com